The Dark Covenant

Occult & Supernatural, Volume 1

Samantha Marie Rodriguez

Published by Serene Sky Publishing, 2024.

This is a work of fiction. Similarities to real people, places, or events are entirely coincidental.

THE DARK COVENANT

First edition. November 24, 2024.

Copyright © 2024 Samantha Marie Rodriguez.

ISBN: 979-8230198031

Written by Samantha Marie Rodriguez.

Table of Contents

Chapter 1: The Invitation 1
Chapter 2: Arrival at Raven's Hollow 10
Chapter 3: The Ancient Ritual 18
Chapter 4: The Forbidden Library 24
Chapter 5: The Shadow Mark 31
Chapter 6: The Blood Moon 38
Chapter 7: The Betrayal 44
Chapter 8: The Lost Manuscript 51
Chapter 9: The Witch's Curse 57
Chapter 10: The Infernal Gate 64
Chapter 11: The Sacrifice 69
Chapter 12: The Final Gathering 74
Chapter 13: The Battle for Souls 80
Chapter 14: The Collapse 86
Chapter 15: The Dawn of Hope 92

To the fearless seekers of truth who venture into the shadows, and to those who stand unwavering in the face of darkness. This book is for the investigative spirits and the brave souls who risk everything to uncover hidden secrets.

And to my family, whose support and belief in the power of storytelling inspire me every day. This journey is dedicated to you.

Chapter 1: The Invitation

Sarah Mitchell's day started like any other: an alarm clock blaring at 6:00 AM, the aroma of freshly brewed coffee filling her modest apartment, and the comforting weight of her well-worn leather satchel resting on her shoulder. As an investigative journalist for one of the city's top newspapers, the **Daily Tribune**, Sarah was no stranger to uncovering hidden truths and exposing the dark underbellies of society. Her life was a whirlwind of deadlines, late-night stakeouts, and the constant buzz of her phone. Yet, despite the chaos, she thrived on the thrill of the chase, the satisfaction of piecing together a story that could change lives.

Sarah's reputation as a relentless and fearless journalist had been built over years of hard work and dedication. She had exposed corrupt politicians, uncovered illegal business practices, and brought to light numerous scandals that others had been too afraid to touch. Her articles were not just words on paper; they were calls to action, pushing the public to demand justice and accountability. However, despite all her accomplishments, Sarah felt a lingering sense of dissatisfaction, a craving for a story that would be her magnum opus—a story that would not just make headlines but would be remembered for years to come.

It was during one of those routine mornings, as she sipped her coffee and skimmed through her overflowing inbox, that she noticed an unusual email. The subject line read: "A Story You Cannot Ignore." Intrigued, she opened the email, which contained only a few lines of text:

"Ms. Mitchell,

There is a story waiting for you in Raven's Hollow. Come alone. It will be the breakthrough you've been searching for.

Regards,

A Friend."

SARAH'S EYEBROWS KNITTED together as she read the message. There was no signature, no contact information, nothing that could give her a clue about the sender. Raven's Hollow was a name she had heard only in whispers, a remote village shrouded in mystery and rumors. According to local folklore, the village was home to a secret society known as the Dark Covenant, a group that practiced ancient rituals and was said to possess dark, otherworldly powers.

Her curiosity piqued, Sarah did what she did best: research. She spent hours digging through online forums, newspaper archives, and any resources she could find on Raven's Hollow and the Dark Covenant. The deeper she dug, the more intrigued she became. The village, located deep in the forested mountains, was isolated from the rest of the world, with no clear records of its population or governance. Accounts from those who had visited were sparse and often conflicting, but one thing was consistent—the mention of the Dark Covenant and their supposed influence over the village.

The more Sarah read, the more she felt the irresistible pull of the unknown. She knew this could be the story she had been searching for, the one that could cement her legacy as a journalist. The mystery of Raven's Hollow and the Dark Covenant was too compelling to ignore.

After a brief meeting with her editor, who reluctantly agreed to let her pursue the lead, Sarah packed her bags and set off for Raven's Hollow. The journey was long and arduous, taking her through winding mountain roads and dense forests. As she drove, she couldn't shake the feeling that she was being watched, an unsettling sensation that only grew stronger the closer she got to the village.

By the time she arrived, the sun was beginning to set, casting long shadows across the narrow, cobblestone streets of Raven's Hollow. The village had an almost timeless quality to it, with its old, weathered buildings and an eerie silence that hung in the air. There were no signs of modern life—no cars, no streetlights, and only a few villagers who quickly looked away when they saw her.

Sarah parked her car at the edge of the village and decided to explore on foot. She walked through the empty streets, her footsteps echoing in the silence. The village seemed almost deserted, with only a few lights flickering in the windows of the houses. She could feel the weight of the villagers' gazes on her, a mixture of curiosity and suspicion.

As she wandered, she came across a small inn. The sign above the door read "The Raven's Nest." Deciding that it would be a good place to start, she pushed open the creaky door and stepped inside. The inn was dimly lit, with a few wooden tables and chairs scattered around the room. A fire crackled in the fireplace, casting a warm glow on the walls.

An elderly woman stood behind the counter, her eyes sharp and piercing. She looked up as Sarah entered, her expression unreadable.

"Good evening," Sarah said, trying to sound casual. "I'm looking for a room for the night."

The woman nodded slowly, her gaze never leaving Sarah's face. "We don't get many visitors here," she said, her voice raspy and low. "What brings you to Raven's Hollow?"

"I'm a journalist," Sarah replied, deciding to be upfront. "I'm here to write a story about the village."

The woman's eyes narrowed slightly, and she seemed to consider Sarah's words for a moment before nodding. "Room's upstairs," she said, sliding a key across the counter. "Last door on the left."

Sarah took the key and thanked the woman before heading up the narrow staircase. The room was small and simple, with a single bed, a wooden dresser, and a window that overlooked the village. She dropped her bags on the floor and sat on the edge of the bed, feeling the weight of the day's journey settle on her shoulders.

As she looked out the window, she saw a figure standing in the shadows, watching her. A chill ran down her spine, but when she blinked, the figure was gone. Shaking off the unsettling feeling, she decided to get some rest. Tomorrow, she would start her investigation into the Dark Covenant and uncover the secrets of Raven's Hollow.

That night, Sarah's sleep was restless, filled with vivid, unsettling dreams. She dreamt of shadowy figures, ancient rituals, and a sense of impending doom. When she woke the next morning, the sun was barely up, and the village was still cloaked in an eerie silence.

Determined to make the most of the day, Sarah set out to explore the village. She walked through the narrow streets, taking in the sights and sounds of Raven's Hollow. The villagers were still wary of her, but she managed to strike up a conversation with a few of them. Most were tight-lipped, offering only vague answers to her questions, but she could sense their fear and suspicion.

It wasn't until she met an elderly man named Thomas that she began to make progress. Thomas had lived in Raven's Hollow his entire life and had seen more than most. He was hesitant at first, but Sarah's persistence paid off, and he eventually agreed to talk.

"The Dark Covenant is real," Thomas said, his voice barely above a whisper. "They've been here for as long as anyone can remember. They control the village, keep us in line. Anyone who tries to leave or speak out against them... they disappear."

Sarah listened intently, her pen scribbling notes furiously. "What can you tell me about their rituals?" she asked.

Thomas glanced around nervously before continuing. "They meet in the forest, near an old stone circle. They perform dark rituals, sacrifices... it's said they can summon spirits, manipulate the weather, even control people's minds."

As Thomas spoke, Sarah felt a sense of unease settle over her. The Dark Covenant sounded more dangerous than she had anticipated. But the more she learned, the more determined she became to uncover the truth.

Armed with the information from Thomas, Sarah decided to visit the stone circle. She hiked through the dense forest, following a narrow, winding path that led to a clearing. The stone circle stood in the center, its weathered stones covered in moss and vines. The air was thick with the scent of damp earth and decay.

Sarah stepped into the circle, feeling a strange energy emanating from the stones. She could almost hear whispers in the wind, voices from the past calling out to her. As she stood there, she noticed something glinting in the grass. Bending down, she picked up a small, silver amulet. It was intricately carved, with symbols she didn't recognize.

She slipped the amulet into her pocket and continued to explore the clearing. There were signs of recent activity—footprints in the mud, remnants of candles, and strange markings on the stones. It was clear that the Dark Covenant had been here recently, and Sarah knew she had to be careful.

As she made her way back to the village, she couldn't shake the feeling that she was being watched. The forest seemed to close in around her, the shadows growing longer and darker. She quickened her pace, her heart pounding in her chest.

When she finally emerged from the forest, she was relieved to see the familiar streets of Raven's Hollow. But her relief was short-lived. As she approached the inn, she saw a group of villagers gathered outside, their expressions grim and hostile.

"You're not welcome here," one of them said, stepping forward. "You need to leave."

Sarah held up her hands in a placating gesture. "I'm just trying to uncover the truth," she said. "I mean no harm."

"The truth is dangerous," the man replied. "And so are you."

Before she could respond, the crowd began to advance, forcing her to back away. She knew she couldn't stay in Raven's Hollow any longer. It was clear that the villagers were under the control of the Dark Covenant, and they would do whatever it took to protect their secrets.

Sarah hurried back to the inn and packed her bags. As she was about to leave, the elderly woman from the night before appeared at the top of the stairs.

"Take this," she said, handing Sarah a small, leather-bound journal. "It belonged to my husband. He was part of the Dark Covenant... before he tried to leave. He wrote everything down. It might help you."

Sarah took the journal, feeling a surge of gratitude. "Thank you," she said. "I'll make sure the truth comes out."

The woman nodded, her eyes filled with sorrow. "Be careful," she said. "The Dark Covenant will stop at nothing to protect their secrets."

With the journal in hand, Sarah left Raven's Hollow, the weight of the villagers' gazes heavy on her back. She knew the road ahead would be dangerous, but she was determined to see her investigation through to the end. The story of the Dark Covenant was too important to ignore, and she wouldn't rest until she had uncovered the truth.

As she drove away from the village, the sun began to set, casting a blood-red glow over the mountains. The amulet in her pocket seemed to pulse with a strange energy, a reminder of the dark forces she was up against. But Sarah was not afraid. She had faced danger before, and she would face it again. The story of Raven's Hollow and the Dark Covenant was just beginning, and she was determined to be the one to tell it.

SARAH SPENT THE NEXT few days poring over the journal the innkeeper had given her. It was filled with detailed accounts of the Dark Covenant's rituals, their history, and their influence over the village. Her husband, John, had been a member of the society, and his writings provided a firsthand look at the darkness that lurked within Raven's Hollow.

One entry, in particular, stood out to Sarah:

"The Dark Covenant is not just a group of individuals seeking power. They are connected to something ancient, something that predates the village itself. The stone circle is a conduit, a gateway to another realm. They use it to harness dark energy, to bend the natural world to their will. I fear for my soul, and for the souls of those who follow them. I must find a way to stop them, to break the cycle of darkness."

JOHN'S WORDS SENT A shiver down Sarah's spine. The implications were staggering. If the Dark Covenant truly had access to otherworldly powers, then the danger they posed was far greater than she had imagined. She needed to find concrete evidence to back up John's claims, something that could expose the society and bring their activities to light.

Determined to continue her investigation, Sarah reached out to a contact she had in the city—a fellow journalist named Mark who specialized in the occult. Mark had helped her with previous stories, and she trusted him to provide valuable insights.

"Raven's Hollow, huh?" Mark said when she called him. "I've heard some pretty wild stories about that place. You're sure you want to go back?"

"I have to," Sarah replied. "There's something big going on there, and I need your help to prove it."

Mark agreed to join her, and they made plans to meet in a nearby town before heading back to Raven's Hollow. Armed with John's journal, the silver amulet, and her determination to uncover the truth, Sarah felt more prepared than ever.

When they arrived at the edge of the village, the sun was beginning to set, casting long shadows across the landscape. Mark's SUV was loaded with equipment—cameras, recording devices, and other tools of the trade. Together, they made their way to the inn, where the elderly woman greeted them with a mixture of relief and apprehension.

"They know you're coming," she said, her voice trembling. "Be careful."

Sarah thanked her and promised to be cautious. With Mark by her side, she felt a renewed sense of purpose. They spent the next few days gathering information, interviewing villagers, and documenting everything they could. The villagers were still wary, but the presence of another outsider seemed to make them more willing to talk.

It wasn't long before they began to uncover disturbing evidence. Strange symbols carved into the walls of houses, hidden caches of ritualistic items, and accounts of bizarre occurrences that defied explanation. Each piece of evidence added to the growing picture of the Dark Covenant's influence over the village.

One evening, as they were reviewing their findings, Mark looked up from his notes. "We need to get inside that stone circle," he said. "That's where the real answers are."

Sarah nodded in agreement. She had been thinking the same thing. The stone circle was the key to understanding the Dark Covenant's power, and they needed to find a way to access it without alerting the society.

They decided to wait for the cover of darkness. Under the light of a full moon, they made their way through the forest, their flashlights cutting through the thick shadows. The air was heavy with anticipation, and every rustle of leaves or snap of a twig set their nerves on edge.

When they reached the clearing, the stone circle stood silent and imposing, bathed in an eerie silver light. Sarah and Mark began to examine the stones, looking for any clues that could help them understand the rituals performed here.

As they worked, Sarah felt a strange energy emanating from the stones. It was as if the air itself was charged with a dark power. She could hear faint whispers, like voices carried on the wind, urging her to leave.

Ignoring the feeling, she continued her search. It wasn't long before they discovered a hidden compartment in one of the stones. Inside, they found a collection of ancient scrolls, written in a language neither of them recognized.

Mark carefully unrolled one of the scrolls, his eyes widening as he read the cryptic symbols. "These are spell incantations," he said, his voice barely above a whisper. "This is powerful stuff, Sarah. We're dealing with real dark magic here."

Sarah's mind raced as she considered the implications. The Dark Covenant wasn't just a group of superstitious villagers—they were practitioners of ancient, dangerous magic. The scrolls were the evidence they needed to expose the society, but they also represented a grave threat.

"We need to get these back to the city," Sarah said. "We have to analyze them, figure out what they mean."

Mark nodded in agreement. "Let's get out of here before they realize we're missing."

As they made their way back through the forest, Sarah couldn't shake the feeling that they were being watched. The trees seemed to close in around them, and the shadows grew darker and more oppressive. They quickened their pace, their breaths coming in short, sharp gasps.

When they finally emerged from the forest, they were both relieved and exhausted. They returned to the inn, where the elderly woman was waiting for them.

"You found something, didn't you?" she asked, her eyes wide with fear and hope.

Sarah nodded. "We found scrolls—spell incantations. This is bigger than we thought."

The woman nodded slowly, her expression grim. "Be careful, child. The Dark Covenant will stop at nothing to protect their secrets."

Sarah thanked her and headed upstairs to her room, clutching the scrolls tightly. She knew they were in possession of something incredibly valuable, but also incredibly dangerous. The Dark Covenant would not take kindly to their intrusion, and they would have to be prepared for whatever came next.

The next morning, Sarah and Mark packed their bags and prepared to leave Raven's Hollow. They had gathered enough evidence to write a groundbreaking story, but they knew they couldn't stay in the village any longer. The Dark Covenant would be watching, and they couldn't risk their lives any further.

As they drove away from the village, Sarah couldn't help but feel a sense of both triumph and trepidation. They had uncovered the truth about the Dark Covenant, but the journey was far from over. The story was just beginning, and she knew it would take all her courage and determination to see it through to the end.

The road ahead was uncertain, and the dangers were real. But Sarah was ready to face them head-on. She had a duty to uncover the truth, to shine a light on the darkness that lurked in Raven's Hollow. And she would not rest until the secrets of the Dark Covenant were exposed for all the world to see.

Chapter 2: Arrival at Raven's Hollow

The drive to Raven's Hollow took Sarah through an increasingly desolate landscape, the road narrowing as the forest on either side grew denser and more foreboding. The sun was beginning to set, casting long shadows that stretched across the cracked asphalt. Sarah's car rattled and bumped along the uneven road, the dense canopy above filtering the last rays of daylight. The GPS on her phone had long since lost signal, and she was relying on a printed map and a sense of direction that was starting to feel more and more uncertain.

Sarah couldn't help but feel a sense of trepidation as she drove deeper into the wilderness. The forest seemed to close in around her, the trees tall and ancient, their gnarled branches reaching out like skeletal hands. Every so often, she thought she saw movement in the underbrush, shadows flitting at the edges of her vision. She shook off the feeling, reminding herself that she was here for a story—a story that could be the biggest of her career.

After what felt like hours, the road finally widened slightly, and the dense forest gave way to a small, dilapidated sign: "Welcome to Raven's Hollow." The sign looked like it hadn't been maintained in decades, its paint peeling and the wood splintered. Sarah pulled over for a moment, taking in the eerie silence. There was no sound of birds, no rustling of leaves—just an oppressive, unnatural quiet.

Taking a deep breath, she started the car again and drove into the village. The houses were old and weathered, many of them seemingly abandoned. The streets were narrow and winding, cobblestone paths that twisted and turned in a way that made the layout of the village feel almost labyrinthine. As she drove, she noticed a few villagers watching her from behind curtains or from the shadows of their doorways. Their eyes were filled with suspicion, their expressions guarded.

Sarah finally found what appeared to be the village square, a small open area with a few benches and an ancient-looking fountain at its center. She parked her car and got out, feeling the eyes of the villagers on her. The air was thick with tension, and she could sense their unease. She was an outsider, and they did not welcome outsiders lightly.

As she stood by her car, trying to get her bearings, an elderly woman approached her. The woman's face was lined with age, her eyes sharp and piercing. She wore a long, dark dress that looked like it had come from another century, and her hands were gnarled and twisted with arthritis.

"You must leave," the woman said, her voice low and urgent. "This is no place for strangers."

Sarah tried to smile, to appear non-threatening. "I'm just here to write a story," she said. "I'm a journalist."

The woman shook her head, her expression hardening. "There are things in this village that are best left alone. If you value your life, you will turn back now."

Before Sarah could respond, the woman turned and walked away, disappearing into the shadows. Sarah felt a chill run down her spine. The warning was clear, and the fear in the woman's eyes was genuine. But Sarah was not one to be easily deterred. She had come too far to turn back now.

Determined to find a place to stay, Sarah headed towards what appeared to be the village inn. The building was old and weathered, like the rest of the village, but it looked more or less maintained. The sign above the door read "The Raven's Nest," and the faint glow of candlelight flickered in the windows.

Sarah pushed open the door and stepped inside. The interior was dimly lit, with a few wooden tables and chairs scattered around the room. A fire crackled in the fireplace, casting a warm glow on the walls. Behind the counter stood an elderly man, his face lined with age and his eyes sharp and watchful.

"Good evening," Sarah said, trying to sound casual. "I'm looking for a room for the night."

The man nodded slowly, his gaze never leaving her face. "We don't get many visitors here," he said, his voice gravelly and low. "What brings you to Raven's Hollow?"

"I'm a journalist," Sarah replied. "I'm here to write a story about the village."

The man's eyes narrowed slightly, and he seemed to consider her words for a moment before nodding. "Room's upstairs," he said, sliding a key across the counter. "Last door on the left."

Sarah took the key and thanked the man before heading up the narrow staircase. The room was small and simple, with a single bed, a wooden dresser, and a window that overlooked the village square. She dropped her bags on the floor and sat on the edge of the bed, feeling the weight of the day's journey settle on her shoulders.

As she looked out the window, she saw a figure standing in the shadows, watching her. A chill ran down her spine, but when she blinked, the figure was gone. Shaking off the unsettling feeling, she decided to get some rest. Tomorrow, she would start her investigation into the Dark Covenant and uncover the secrets of Raven's Hollow.

The next morning, Sarah woke early, eager to begin her work. She dressed quickly and headed downstairs, where the innkeeper was preparing breakfast. He glanced up as she entered the room, his expression unreadable.

"Do you know where I can find more information about the village?" Sarah asked as she poured herself a cup of coffee.

The innkeeper shrugged. "Depends on what you're looking for," he said. "But most folks around here don't take kindly to strangers asking too many questions."

Sarah nodded, her resolve hardening. "I'll keep that in mind," she said. "Thanks."

After a quick breakfast, she left the inn and began to explore the village. The streets were still eerily quiet, the air thick with an unspoken tension. As she walked, she noticed more of the strange, secretive villagers, their eyes following her every move. Despite their warnings, she knew she had to push forward.

As she wandered through the narrow streets, she eventually came across a small, dilapidated building that looked like it might have once been a library. The windows were dirty and cracked, and the door hung slightly ajar. Curiosity getting the better of her, Sarah pushed the door open and stepped inside.

The interior was dusty and dimly lit, with rows of old, musty books lining the shelves. As she moved further into the room, she heard a rustling sound and turned to see an elderly man hunched over a table, examining a large, leather-bound book. His hair was white and unkempt, and his clothes were worn and tattered.

"Excuse me," Sarah said, trying not to startle him. "I'm looking for information about the village. Can you help me?"

The man looked up, his eyes sharp and penetrating. He studied her for a moment before nodding slowly. "You're the journalist," he said, his voice raspy. "I've been expecting you."

Sarah raised an eyebrow. "You have?"

The man nodded again. "The village has a way of knowing when someone new arrives. I suppose you're here about the Dark Covenant."

Sarah's heart skipped a beat at the mention of the secret society. "Yes," she said, stepping closer. "What can you tell me about them?"

The man sighed and closed the book he was reading. "The Dark Covenant has been a part of this village for as long as anyone can remember," he said. "They practice ancient rituals, dark magic, things that most people wouldn't believe. They hold the village in their grip, controlling everything from behind the scenes."

Sarah listened intently, her pen scribbling notes furiously. "Do you know where they meet?" she asked.

The man hesitated, glancing around the room as if afraid of being overheard. "There's a stone circle in the forest," he said finally. "That's where they perform their rituals. But be careful—if they catch you, they'll do whatever it takes to protect their secrets."

Sarah nodded, feeling a mix of excitement and apprehension. She had a lead, and it was more than she had expected to find so quickly. "Thank you," she said. "I'll be careful."

As she left the building, she couldn't shake the feeling that she was being watched. The villagers' eyes seemed to follow her every move, their expressions wary and hostile. She knew she had to tread carefully, but she was determined to uncover the truth.

Her next stop was the village market, a small, open-air space with a few stalls selling fruits, vegetables, and handmade goods. The vendors eyed her suspiciously as she walked by, but she managed to strike up a conversation with a woman selling herbs and spices.

"Do you know anything about the Dark Covenant?" Sarah asked, keeping her voice low.

The woman's eyes widened, and she glanced around nervously. "You shouldn't be asking about them," she whispered. "It's dangerous."

"I need to know the truth," Sarah said. "Please, anything you can tell me would be helpful."

The woman hesitated, then leaned in closer. "They meet in the forest, near an old stone circle," she said. "They perform dark rituals, sacrifices... it's said they can summon spirits, manipulate the weather, even control people's minds. But you didn't hear that from me."

Sarah thanked the woman and made her way back to the inn, her mind racing with the information she had gathered. The Dark Covenant was more powerful and dangerous than she had imagined, and she knew she had to be careful. But she was also more determined than ever to uncover their secrets and bring them to light.

As she approached the inn, she saw a man standing outside, leaning against the wall with his arms crossed. He was tall and lean, with dark hair and piercing blue eyes. He watched her with an intensity that made her heart skip a beat.

"You're the journalist," he said as she drew closer. "I've been waiting for you."

Sarah frowned, her curiosity piqued. "And you are?"

"Ethan," the man replied, pushing himself off the wall. "I can help you find what you're looking for."

Sarah studied him for a moment, unsure whether to trust him. "And why would you want to help me?"

Ethan shrugged. "Let's just say I have my reasons," he said. "The Dark Covenant has been a blight on this village for too long. It's time someone did something about it."

Sarah felt a spark of hope. "Alright," she said. "What do you know about the Dark Covenant?"

Ethan glanced around, making sure they weren't being overheard. "A lot more than most people in this village," he said. "But we can't talk here. Meet me at the old church tonight. I'll tell you everything you need to know."

With that, he turned and walked away, leaving Sarah with more questions than answers. She watched him go, her mind racing. Ethan was an enigma, and she couldn't be sure of his motives. But he seemed genuine, and she needed all the help she could get.

That evening, as the sun began to set, Sarah made her way to the old church on the outskirts of the village. The building was dilapidated and overgrown with ivy, its once-grand facade now crumbling and decayed. She pushed open the heavy wooden door and stepped inside, her footsteps echoing in the empty space.

Ethan was waiting for her near the altar, a lantern casting a warm glow on his features. He looked up as she approached, his expression serious.

"You're here," he said. "Good."

Sarah nodded. "You said you could help me. What do you know about the Dark Covenant?"

Ethan took a deep breath, his gaze distant. "The Dark Covenant is not just a group of villagers practicing dark magic," he said. "They're connected to something much older and more powerful. The stone circle in the forest is a gateway to another realm, a place where dark forces dwell. They use it to harness that power, to control the village and anyone who stands in their way."

Sarah's eyes widened. "And you know this how?"

Ethan hesitated, then reached into his pocket and pulled out a small, silver amulet. It was intricately carved, with symbols that matched the ones Sarah had seen in the library. "Because I was once one of them," he said quietly. "I left when I realized the true extent of their power. But I've been watching them ever since, trying to find a way to stop them."

Sarah felt a chill run down her spine. Ethan's revelation was both shocking and terrifying. "Why are you telling me this?" she asked.

"Because you have a chance to expose them," Ethan said. "To bring their activities to light and put an end to their reign of terror. But you have to be careful. They're always watching, always listening. One wrong move, and they'll know."

Sarah nodded, her resolve hardening. "What do I need to do?"

Ethan glanced around, his expression tense. "Meet me tomorrow night at the stone circle," he said. "I'll show you what you need to see. But be prepared. Once you go down this path, there's no turning back."

Sarah agreed, her mind racing with the implications of Ethan's words. She had come to Raven's Hollow looking for a story, but she had found something much more dangerous. The Dark Covenant was real, and their power was far greater than she had imagined. But with Ethan's help, she might just have a chance to uncover the truth and bring them down.

As she left the church and made her way back to the inn, she couldn't shake the feeling that she was being watched. The village seemed even more oppressive in the darkness, the shadows deeper and more menacing. But she pushed her fear aside, focusing on the task ahead.

The next day passed in a blur as Sarah prepared for her meeting with Ethan. She gathered her notes, her camera, and anything else she thought she might need. As night fell, she made her way to the edge of the forest, her heart pounding in her chest.

Ethan was waiting for her, his expression serious. "Are you ready?" he asked.

Sarah nodded, steeling herself for what lay ahead. "Let's do this."

Together, they made their way through the dense forest, the path winding and treacherous. The air was thick with tension, and every rustle of leaves or snap of a twig set Sarah's nerves on edge. But she pressed on, determined to see her investigation through.

When they finally reached the clearing, the stone circle stood silent and imposing, bathed in the eerie light of the full moon. Ethan led her to the center of the circle, where the energy seemed to hum with a dark, palpable power.

"This is where they perform their rituals," Ethan said, his voice barely above a whisper. "This is where they harness the power of the other realm."

Sarah looked around, her heart racing. The stone circle felt alive with a dark energy, and she could almost hear the whispers of ancient voices. She knew she was standing on the precipice of something huge, something that could change everything.

As she began to document the scene, taking photos and jotting down notes, she couldn't shake the feeling that they were being watched. The shadows seemed to move of their own accord, and the air grew colder with each passing moment.

Suddenly, Ethan grabbed her arm, his expression urgent. "We need to go," he said. "They're coming."

Before Sarah could react, they were running through the forest, the sounds of pursuit close behind them. Her heart pounded in her chest as she stumbled over roots and branches, her breath coming in short, ragged gasps.

When they finally emerged from the forest, they didn't stop until they reached the safety of the village. Sarah's mind was racing, the events of the night playing over and over in her head. She had seen the power of the Dark Covenant firsthand, and she knew she had to expose them.

As she caught her breath, Ethan turned to her, his expression grim. "Now you know," he said. "Now you see what we're up against."

Sarah nodded, her resolve stronger than ever. She had come to Raven's Hollow looking for a story, but she had found something much more dangerous. With Ethan's help, she would uncover the truth and bring the Dark Covenant to light. But she knew the road ahead would be treacherous, and the stakes higher than she had ever imagined.

The village of Raven's Hollow was shrouded in darkness, its secrets hidden in the shadows. But Sarah was determined to shine a light on that darkness, to uncover the truth and bring justice to those who had suffered under the Dark Covenant's reign. The journey ahead would be perilous, but she was ready to face whatever came her way.

With Ethan by her side, she felt a glimmer of hope. Together, they would unravel the mysteries of Raven's Hollow and expose the dark forces at play. And in the end, they would bring the truth to light, no matter the cost.

Chapter 3: The Ancient Ritual

Sarah spent the next morning reviewing her notes and photographs from the previous night. The images of the stone circle and the eerie atmosphere it evoked were vivid reminders of the dangers she faced. She knew that to understand the true nature of the Dark Covenant, she needed to delve deeper into their history and rituals. Her conversation with Ethan had opened the door to a world she barely understood, and she needed more information to piece together the full picture.

As she sat in the dimly lit room of the inn, her mind wandered back to the elderly man in the library. His knowledge had been invaluable, and she hoped he might be able to shed more light on the rituals performed by the Dark Covenant. With renewed determination, she set out to find him again.

The village was quiet as she made her way to the old library, the morning fog still lingering in the air. The building looked even more decrepit in the daylight, its windows dark and foreboding. Sarah pushed open the door and stepped inside, the musty smell of old books and dust filling her nostrils.

The elderly man was in the same spot as before, hunched over a table with a stack of ancient texts. He looked up as she approached, his eyes narrowing in recognition.

"You're back," he said, his voice raspy. "I take it you found what you were looking for last night."

Sarah nodded. "I did, but I need to know more," she said. "I need to understand the rituals they perform and their significance."

The man sighed, closing the book he had been reading. "The rituals of the Dark Covenant are ancient, passed down through generations," he said. "They are rooted in dark magic and the invocation of otherworldly entities. These rituals are what give the Covenant its power, and they are not to be taken lightly."

Sarah pulled out her notebook and pen, ready to take notes. "Can you tell me about one of these rituals?" she asked. "Something that would give me a better understanding of what I'm dealing with."

The man hesitated for a moment, then nodded. "There is one ritual in particular that stands out," he said. "It is known as the Rite of Ascension. This ritual is performed only once every few decades, and it is said to grant the Covenant's leader immense power. The Rite involves the sacrifice of a chosen individual, whose blood is used to open a gateway to the other realm."

Sarah's heart raced as she listened. The gravity of what she was uncovering was immense. "Do you know when the next Rite of Ascension is supposed to take place?" she asked.

The man shook his head. "I do not know the exact date, but I believe it is soon," he said. "The signs are all there—the increased activity in the village, the heightened tension among the villagers. The Covenant is preparing for something big."

Sarah thanked the man for his information and left the library, her mind racing with the implications of what she had learned. The Rite of Ascension was a pivotal event for the Dark Covenant, and if she could witness it, she might be able to gather the evidence she needed to expose them.

That evening, she met Ethan at the edge of the village. He was waiting for her, his expression serious.

"I spoke with the librarian again," Sarah said. "He told me about a ritual called the Rite of Ascension. Do you know anything about it?"

Ethan's face darkened. "I do," he said. "The Rite of Ascension is one of the most powerful and dangerous rituals the Covenant performs. If they're planning to conduct it soon, we need to stop them."

Sarah nodded. "We need to witness it," she said. "We need to gather evidence and document everything."

Ethan agreed, and they made their way to the forest, following the same path they had taken the night before. The air was thick with anticipation, and every rustle of leaves or snap of a twig set their nerves on edge.

As they approached the stone circle, they heard the faint sound of chanting. The clearing was bathed in the light of torches, and the shadows of robed figures danced across the stones. Sarah and Ethan hid behind a large tree, peering out to watch the ritual unfold.

The members of the Dark Covenant stood in a circle, their faces hidden by hoods. In the center of the circle lay a young woman, bound and gagged. Her eyes were wide with fear, and she struggled against her restraints.

The leader of the Covenant, a tall man with an air of authority, stepped forward. He held a ceremonial dagger in his hand, its blade glinting in the torchlight. He began to chant in a language Sarah didn't recognize, his voice rising and falling in a rhythmic pattern.

As the chanting grew louder, the air around them seemed to vibrate with energy. The torches flickered, and the shadows deepened. Sarah felt a chill run down her spine as the leader raised the dagger, his eyes fixed on the bound woman.

Just as he was about to bring the dagger down, a figure burst into the clearing, shouting. It was the elderly librarian, his face filled with determination and fear.

"Stop this madness!" he cried. "You don't know what you're doing!"

The members of the Covenant turned to face him, their expressions hidden by their hoods. The leader sneered, his grip on the dagger tightening.

"You dare to interrupt our sacred ritual?" he hissed. "You have no idea of the power we wield."

The librarian stood his ground, his eyes blazing with defiance. "I know enough," he said. "I know that you are playing with forces beyond your control. This ritual will bring nothing but destruction."

Sarah watched in horror as the leader raised the dagger again, this time aiming it at the librarian. Before she could react, Ethan grabbed her arm, pulling her back into the shadows.

"We need to go," he whispered urgently. "Now."

Reluctantly, Sarah allowed herself to be led away, her heart pounding in her chest. As they ran through the forest, the sounds of the ritual and the librarian's desperate cries echoed in her ears. She knew she had to do something, but she also knew that confronting the Covenant head-on was too dangerous.

When they finally reached the safety of the village, Sarah turned to Ethan, her mind racing with questions.

"What do we do now?" she asked, her voice trembling. "How do we stop them?"

Ethan took a deep breath, his expression resolute. "We need to find out more about the Rite of Ascension," he said. "There has to be a way to disrupt the ritual, to break the Covenant's hold on the village."

Sarah nodded, her determination renewed. She had witnessed the power of the Dark Covenant firsthand, and she knew that stopping them would not be easy. But with Ethan's help, she was determined to uncover the truth and put an end to their dark reign.

Over the next few days, Sarah and Ethan delved deeper into the history of the Dark Covenant. They pored over ancient texts, spoke to villagers who were willing to share their stories, and pieced together the dark origins of the society.

The Dark Covenant had been founded centuries ago by a group of villagers who sought to harness the power of the other realm. They believed that through dark rituals and sacrifices, they could gain control over natural forces and bend them to their will. Over time, the Covenant grew in power and influence, and their rituals became more elaborate and dangerous.

One of the key figures in the Covenant's history was a man named Elias Blackwood. He had been the leader of the Covenant during a time of great upheaval and had been responsible for many of the society's most notorious rituals. Elias had been a charismatic and ruthless leader, and his influence still lingered in the village.

Flashbacks revealed the dark history of the Covenant, showing the lengths to which they had gone to maintain their power. Villagers who had opposed them were silenced, and those who had tried to leave the society met with mysterious and often deadly accidents. The Covenant's grip on the village was absolute, and their influence reached far beyond the borders of Raven's Hollow.

As Sarah learned more about the Covenant's history, she began to understand the depth of their power and the danger they posed. The Rite of Ascension was just one of many rituals they performed, each designed to strengthen their connection to the other realm and increase their control over the village.

Determined to disrupt the upcoming ritual, Sarah and Ethan continued their investigation. They discovered that the Rite of Ascension required specific elements to be successful—a sacrificial victim, a ceremonial dagger, and a series of incantations that had to be performed in a precise order. If any of these elements were missing or disrupted, the ritual would fail.

Armed with this knowledge, Sarah and Ethan devised a plan to stop the Covenant. They would infiltrate the ritual, disrupt the incantations, and rescue the sacrificial victim. It was a risky plan, but it was their only hope of stopping the Covenant and saving the village.

The night of the ritual arrived, and Sarah and Ethan made their way to the stone circle, their hearts pounding with anticipation. The air was thick with tension, and the forest seemed to come alive with shadows and whispers.

As they approached the clearing, they saw the members of the Covenant gathered around the stone circle, their torches casting an eerie glow. The young woman lay bound in the center, her eyes wide with fear.

Sarah and Ethan moved silently through the underbrush, positioning themselves close enough to the circle to hear the incantations. The leader of the Covenant stepped forward, his voice rising in a rhythmic chant.

Ethan nodded to Sarah, and she took a deep breath, steeling herself for what was to come. As the leader raised the ceremonial dagger, she sprang into action, shouting to distract him.

"Stop!" she cried, her voice echoing through the clearing. "You don't have to do this!"

The leader's eyes widened in surprise, and the chanting faltered. Ethan took advantage of the distraction, rushing forward to grab the dagger from the leader's hand. Chaos erupted as the members of the Covenant reacted, their hoods falling back to reveal their shocked faces.

Sarah moved quickly to the center of the circle, untying the young woman and helping her to her feet. The girl was trembling, her eyes filled with gratitude and fear.

"Run!" Sarah urged her. "Get out of here and don't look back."

The girl nodded and took off into the forest, her footsteps echoing in the night. Sarah turned to see Ethan struggling with the leader, the two men locked in a fierce battle for control of the dagger.

With a burst of strength, Ethan managed to disarm the leader, throwing the dagger into the underbrush. The chanting had stopped, and the air seemed to crackle with a sense of impending doom.

"We need to go, now!" Ethan shouted, grabbing Sarah's hand.

They ran through the forest, the sounds of pursuit close behind them. The members of the Covenant were relentless, their footsteps pounding in the darkness. But Sarah and Ethan were determined to escape, to put an end to the Covenant's dark reign once and for all.

When they finally emerged from the forest, they didn't stop until they reached the village. The innkeeper was waiting for them, his expression a mixture of fear and relief.

"You did it," he said, his voice trembling. "You stopped them."

Sarah nodded, her heart still racing. "We did, but it's not over yet," she said. "We need to expose them, to make sure they can never hurt anyone again."

With the evidence they had gathered and the testimonies of the villagers who had witnessed the Covenant's dark rituals, Sarah and Ethan set out to bring the truth to light. They contacted authorities, journalists, and anyone who would listen, determined to expose the dark secrets of Raven's Hollow.

The village slowly began to change as the truth came to light. The members of the Covenant were arrested and brought to justice, their power finally broken. The villagers who had lived in fear for so long began to rebuild their lives, free from the shadow of the Covenant.

As the days turned into weeks and the weeks into months, Sarah and Ethan remained in Raven's Hollow, helping the villagers heal and documenting the transformation. Their bond grew stronger as they worked together, their shared experiences forging a deep connection.

In the end, Sarah had found more than just a story—she had found a purpose, a calling to uncover the truth and bring justice to those who needed it most. And with Ethan by her side, she knew they could face whatever challenges lay ahead.

The Dark Covenant was no more, but the lessons learned and the bonds forged in the fight against darkness would endure. Sarah and Ethan had uncovered the truth, and in doing so, they had brought light to the darkest corners of Raven's Hollow.

Chapter 4: The Forbidden Library

The events of the past few days had left Sarah feeling a mixture of exhilaration and exhaustion. The village of Raven's Hollow had finally begun to shed some of its oppressive darkness, but the work was far from over. As Sarah sat in her room at the inn, she reviewed the notes she had taken and the photographs she had snapped. There was still so much she didn't understand about the Dark Covenant and their rituals, and she knew that she needed more information to piece together the full story.

That morning, Sarah decided to pay another visit to the village's old library. The librarian had been an invaluable source of information, and Sarah hoped that he might have more to share. As she walked through the village, the fog still clung to the ground, casting an eerie pall over the narrow streets. The villagers, while more open to her presence now, still regarded her with a mixture of wariness and curiosity.

When Sarah reached the library, she found the door slightly ajar, just as it had been before. She stepped inside, the familiar scent of old books and dust greeting her. The librarian was at his usual spot, hunched over a table with a stack of ancient texts. He looked up as she approached, his eyes narrowing in recognition.

"Back again?" he said, his voice raspy. "I take it you've come for more answers."

Sarah nodded. "I need to understand more about the Dark Covenant and their rituals," she said. "There are still so many unanswered questions."

The librarian sighed and closed the book he had been reading. "You've already uncovered more than most outsiders ever do," he said. "But if you're determined to continue, there is one place that might have the answers you seek."

Sarah's curiosity was piqued. "Where?" she asked.

The librarian hesitated for a moment before speaking. "There is a hidden library beneath this building," he said. "It was created centuries ago by the founders of the village, and it contains texts that are far older and more dangerous than anything you'll find up here. But be warned—what you find there could change everything."

Sarah's heart raced with anticipation. "How do I get there?" she asked.

The librarian stood and walked to the far corner of the room, where a large, dusty bookshelf stood against the wall. He pulled a lever hidden behind one of the books, and the bookshelf swung open to reveal a dark, narrow staircase leading down into the depths of the building.

"Follow the stairs," he said. "But be careful. The knowledge contained in the forbidden library is powerful, and it has driven many to madness."

Sarah took a deep breath and stepped onto the staircase. As she descended, the air grew colder, and the darkness seemed to press in around her. The walls were lined with ancient, crumbling stones, and the only light came from a flickering torch mounted on the wall at the bottom of the stairs.

When she reached the bottom, she found herself in a small, dimly lit room. Shelves lined the walls, filled with books and scrolls that looked as though they hadn't been touched in centuries. A large, ornate table stood in the center of the room, and on it lay an open book, its pages filled with strange, arcane symbols.

Sarah approached the table and began to examine the book. The symbols were unlike anything she had ever seen, and she couldn't make sense of them. As she flipped through the pages, she noticed a passage written in a language she could understand. It spoke of a prophecy tied to the Dark Covenant, a prophecy that foretold the rise of a great darkness and the coming of a chosen one who would either save the village or doom it to eternal night.

Her hands trembled as she read the words. The prophecy spoke of a series of rituals that would culminate in the Rite of Ascension, and it hinted at the possibility of disrupting the ritual and breaking the Covenant's hold on the village. But it also warned of the dangers of meddling with forces beyond comprehension, and it hinted at a great sacrifice that would be required to bring about the prophecy's fulfillment.

As Sarah absorbed the information, she heard a soft rustling sound behind her. She turned to see an old woman standing in the doorway, her eyes filled with a mix of wisdom and sorrow. The woman was dressed in a long, flowing robe, and her hair was a wild tangle of silver strands.

"Who are you?" Sarah asked, her voice barely above a whisper.

The woman stepped into the room, her gaze never leaving Sarah's face. "I am the keeper of this library," she said. "My name is Elara. I have been watching over these texts for longer than you can imagine."

Sarah felt a chill run down her spine. "You know about the prophecy," she said.

Elara nodded. "I do. And I know why you are here. You seek to uncover the truth and bring an end to the Dark Covenant."

Sarah nodded, her determination unwavering. "I need to know more," she said. "I need to understand the rituals and the prophecy if I am to have any chance of stopping them."

Elara sighed and walked over to the table, her fingers gently brushing the pages of the open book. "The prophecy is ancient, and its origins are shrouded in mystery," she said. "It speaks of a chosen one who will either save the village or doom it to eternal darkness. The chosen one is marked by a unique birthmark, a symbol of their destiny."

Sarah's mind raced as she processed the information. "Do you know who the chosen one is?" she asked.

Elara shook her head. "The identity of the chosen one has been lost to time," she said. "But the prophecy also speaks of a great sacrifice that must be made to disrupt the Rite of Ascension and break the Covenant's hold on the village. The sacrifice is not just physical, but also spiritual—a test of the chosen one's strength and resolve."

Sarah's heart sank at the thought of the sacrifice. "Is there no other way?" she asked.

Elara's eyes were filled with sorrow. "The path you have chosen is fraught with danger," she said. "The knowledge contained in these texts is powerful, but it is also dangerous. Many who have sought to use it have been consumed by it."

Sarah took a deep breath, steeling herself for what lay ahead. "I have to try," she said. "I can't let the Dark Covenant continue their reign of terror."

Elara nodded, her expression resigned. "Very well," she said. "But be warned—once you start down this path, there is no turning back."

With Elara's guidance, Sarah spent the next several hours poring over the ancient texts. The books were filled with detailed descriptions of the rituals performed by the Dark Covenant, as well as the incantations and symbols used to invoke the otherworldly entities they sought to control.

As she read, Sarah began to piece together a plan. The prophecy spoke of a series of elements that were crucial to the success of the Rite of Ascension—a sacrificial victim, a ceremonial dagger, and a series of incantations that had to be performed in a precise order. If any of these elements were disrupted, the ritual would fail.

Sarah knew that she and Ethan would need to act quickly and decisively to disrupt the ritual. They would need to find the ceremonial dagger and replace it with a replica, disrupt the incantations, and rescue the sacrificial victim before the ritual could be completed.

As she absorbed the information, Elara watched her with a mixture of concern and admiration. "You are brave to undertake this quest," she said. "But remember—knowledge is a double-edged sword. Use it wisely, and do not underestimate the power of the Dark Covenant."

Sarah nodded, her resolve unwavering. "I will," she said. "Thank you for your help."

Elara gave her a sad smile. "May the fates be with you," she said.

With the knowledge she had gained, Sarah made her way back up the narrow staircase and out of the library. The sun was beginning to set, casting long shadows across the village. As she walked through the streets, she couldn't shake the feeling that she was being watched.

When she reached the inn, she found Ethan waiting for her. His expression was tense, and he looked as though he hadn't slept in days.

"Did you find what you were looking for?" he asked.

Sarah nodded and quickly filled him in on what she had learned. Ethan listened intently, his face growing more serious with each passing moment.

"We need to move quickly," he said when she had finished. "If the prophecy is correct, we don't have much time before the Rite of Ascension is performed."

Sarah agreed, and they set to work on their plan. They spent the next several days gathering the materials they would need, including a replica of the ceremonial dagger and the tools to disrupt the incantations.

As the night of the ritual approached, the tension in the village grew palpable. The villagers were on edge, and the members of the Dark Covenant were more vigilant than ever. Sarah and Ethan knew that they had to be careful, but they also knew that they couldn't afford to fail.

The night of the ritual arrived, and Sarah and Ethan made their way to the stone circle. The air was thick with anticipation, and the forest seemed to come alive with shadows and whispers. They hid in the underbrush, watching as the members of the Covenant gathered around the circle, their torches casting an eerie glow.

The leader of the Covenant stepped forward, holding the ceremonial dagger aloft. He began to chant in a rhythmic pattern, his voice rising and falling with each incantation. The air around them seemed to vibrate with energy, and the torches flickered as though caught in an unseen wind.

Sarah and Ethan moved quickly, their hearts pounding with adrenaline. They swapped the ceremonial dagger with the replica and began to disrupt the incantations, their movements swift and precise. The leader of the Covenant seemed oblivious to their actions, his focus entirely on the ritual.

As the chanting grew louder, Sarah felt a strange energy emanating from the stone circle. The air crackled with power, and the shadows deepened. She glanced at Ethan, who gave her a reassuring nod.

Just as the leader was about to complete the final incantation, Sarah sprang into action, shouting to distract him. The chanting faltered, and the members of the Covenant turned to face her, their expressions hidden by their hoods.

"Stop this madness!" Sarah cried. "You don't know what you're doing!"

The leader's eyes widened in surprise, and for a moment, the air was filled with an eerie silence. Then, chaos erupted. The members of the Covenant rushed forward, trying to apprehend Sarah and Ethan. But the disruption of the ritual had already taken its toll.

The ground beneath the stone circle began to tremble, and a blinding light erupted from the center. The energy that had been building throughout the ritual was unleashed in a powerful wave, knocking the members of the Covenant to the ground.

Sarah and Ethan took advantage of the chaos to rescue the sacrificial victim, a young woman who had been bound and gagged at the center of the circle. They untied her and helped her to her feet, urging her to run.

"Go!" Sarah shouted. "Get out of here and don't look back!"

The girl nodded, tears streaming down her face, and took off into the forest. Sarah and Ethan followed close behind, their hearts pounding with a mixture of fear and exhilaration.

When they finally reached the safety of the village, they didn't stop until they were inside the inn. The villagers had gathered outside, their expressions a mixture of fear and confusion.

"What happened?" one of them asked.

Sarah took a deep breath, her heart still racing. "We disrupted the ritual," she said. "The Dark Covenant's hold on this village is broken."

The villagers stared at her in disbelief, their expressions slowly transforming into relief and gratitude. The oppressive darkness that had hung over Raven's Hollow for so long began to lift, and the air seemed to grow lighter.

Over the next several days, Sarah and Ethan helped the villagers rebuild their lives. The members of the Covenant who had survived the disruption of the ritual were brought to justice, and the village began to heal.

Sarah knew that their journey was far from over. There were still many unanswered questions, and the threat of the Dark Covenant was not entirely gone. But for now, they had won a significant victory.

As the days turned into weeks and the weeks into months, Sarah and Ethan remained in Raven's Hollow, documenting the transformation and helping the villagers reclaim their lives. Their bond grew stronger, forged by the shared experiences and the challenges they had faced together.

In the end, Sarah had found more than just a story—she had found a purpose, a calling to uncover the truth and bring justice to those who needed it most. And with Ethan by her side, she knew they could face whatever challenges lay ahead.

The forbidden library had been a source of great knowledge and power, but it had also been a reminder of the dangers of seeking the truth. Sarah had learned to wield that knowledge wisely, and she knew that the journey ahead would be filled with both light and darkness.

With the prophecy in mind and the support of her newfound allies, Sarah was ready to face whatever the future held. The Dark Covenant may have been defeated, but the lessons learned and the bonds forged in the fight against darkness would endure.

Sarah and Ethan had uncovered the truth, and in doing so, they had brought light to the darkest corners of Raven's Hollow. The village had begun to heal, and a new era of hope and resilience had dawned.

As Sarah looked out over the village from the window of her room at the inn, she felt a sense of peace and fulfillment. The journey had been long and difficult, but it had also been worth it. She had found the story she had been searching for, and in the process, she had found herself.

The road ahead would undoubtedly bring new challenges and adventures, but Sarah was ready to face them head-on. With Ethan by her side and the support of the villagers, she knew that they could overcome any obstacle.

The forbidden library had opened her eyes to a world of ancient secrets and dark powers, but it had also shown her the strength of the human spirit and the power of resilience. As she closed the book she had been reading and looked out at the rising sun, she knew that the journey was only just beginning.

And with that thought, she turned to face the future with hope and determination, ready to uncover the truth and bring light to the darkest corners of the world.

Chapter 5: The Shadow Mark

Sarah's sleep was restless, filled with vivid, unsettling dreams. She found herself in a dark forest, the moonlight barely penetrating the dense canopy of trees. The air was thick and cold, and every sound seemed amplified in the eerie silence. Shadows moved at the edge of her vision, and she felt an overwhelming sense of being watched. As she walked deeper into the forest, she came upon a clearing with a stone circle, much like the one she had seen in Raven's Hollow. In the center of the circle stood a figure, cloaked in darkness, its eyes glowing with an otherworldly light.

The figure raised a hand, and Sarah felt a searing pain on her right shoulder. She tried to scream, but no sound came out. The pain intensified, spreading through her body, and she woke up with a start, drenched in sweat and gasping for breath.

She lay in bed for a few moments, trying to shake off the lingering fear from the dream. Her shoulder still ached, and she reached up to touch it, feeling a strange, raised mark on her skin. She bolted out of bed and rushed to the mirror. There, on her right shoulder, was a dark, intricate symbol that she had never seen before.

Panic set in as she stared at the mark. She had no idea how it had gotten there or what it meant. Her mind raced with possibilities, but one thing was clear: this was no ordinary mark. She needed answers, and she needed them fast.

Sarah quickly dressed and left her room, heading straight for Ethan's. She knocked urgently on his door, and it opened almost immediately. Ethan stood there, looking concerned.

"Sarah, what's wrong?" he asked.

Without a word, she pulled down the collar of her shirt to reveal the mark on her shoulder. Ethan's eyes widened in shock and recognition.

"Come in," he said, his voice tense.

Sarah entered the room, and Ethan closed the door behind her. She could see the worry in his eyes as he studied the mark.

"What is it?" she asked, her voice trembling.

Ethan took a deep breath. "It's a shadow mark," he said. "A sign that you've been chosen by the Dark Covenant."

Sarah's heart skipped a beat. "Chosen for what?" she asked.

"The mark signifies that you are connected to the prophecy," Ethan explained. "The Dark Covenant believes that you are the chosen one who will either save the village or doom it to eternal darkness."

Sarah felt a wave of fear wash over her. "But why me?" she asked. "I didn't ask for this."

"The prophecy is ancient," Ethan said. "It speaks of a chosen one who will bear the shadow mark and play a pivotal role in the fate of the village. The mark appeared on you because you are meant to fulfill that role, whether you want to or not."

Sarah felt overwhelmed by the weight of this revelation. She had come to Raven's Hollow to uncover the truth about the Dark Covenant, but now she was entangled in a prophecy that could determine the fate of the entire village.

"We need to find out more about this mark and what it means for you," Ethan said. "There's a local witch who might be able to help us. She knows more about the old ways and the prophecy than anyone else in the village."

Sarah nodded, grateful for Ethan's support. "Let's go," she said. "I need to understand what's happening to me."

They left the inn and made their way through the village, heading towards the edge of the forest where the witch was said to live. The villagers watched them with a mixture of curiosity and suspicion, but Sarah was too focused on finding answers to care.

As they walked, Sarah couldn't help but feel a growing sense of unease. The mark on her shoulder seemed to pulse with a strange energy, and she could almost hear faint whispers in the wind. She tried to push the feeling aside, but it lingered, gnawing at the edges of her mind.

They reached a small, secluded cottage at the edge of the forest. The air around the cottage felt thick and charged with an unfamiliar energy. Ethan knocked on the door, and after a few moments, it creaked open to reveal an elderly woman with piercing blue eyes and long, silver hair.

"Ethan," the woman said, her voice soft but commanding. "What brings you here?"

"We need your help, Selene," Ethan said. "This is Sarah. She's been marked by the Dark Covenant."

Selene's eyes narrowed as she looked at Sarah. "Come inside," she said, stepping aside to let them in.

The inside of the cottage was cluttered with herbs, jars, and strange trinkets. A large, wooden table dominated the center of the room, covered with an assortment of books and candles. Selene motioned for them to sit, and she took a seat across from them.

"Show me the mark," she said.

Sarah pulled down the collar of her shirt to reveal the mark on her shoulder. Selene leaned in, studying it closely. Her expression grew more serious with each passing moment.

"This is indeed a shadow mark," she said finally. "A powerful and ancient symbol tied to the prophecy. It signifies that you are the chosen one, and your fate is intertwined with the fate of this village."

Sarah felt a shiver run down her spine. "What does it mean for me?" she asked. "What am I supposed to do?"

Selene sighed and leaned back in her chair. "The prophecy speaks of a great darkness that will descend upon the village, and a chosen one who will either save it or doom it," she said. "The mark indicates that you have been chosen to fulfill this role. But the path you must take is not clear. There are many trials ahead, and the choices you make will determine the outcome."

Sarah's mind raced with questions. "What kind of trials?" she asked. "And how do I know what choices to make?"

Selene gave her a sad smile. "The path of the chosen one is fraught with danger and uncertainty," she said. "You will be tested in ways you cannot imagine. The mark on your shoulder is both a blessing and a curse. It grants you certain abilities, but it also makes you a target for the dark forces that seek to control you."

Sarah felt a lump form in her throat. "What kind of abilities?" she asked.

"The mark connects you to the other realm," Selene explained. "It allows you to tap into the ancient magic that the Dark Covenant seeks to harness. But using this power comes at a great cost. It can consume you if you're not careful."

Sarah took a deep breath, trying to process everything she had just learned. "How do I control it?" she asked.

Selene reached into a drawer and pulled out a small, silver amulet. "This amulet will help you focus your abilities," she said, handing it to Sarah. "Wear it at all times, and it will protect you from the dark forces that seek to harm you."

Sarah took the amulet and slipped it around her neck. She felt a strange warmth spread through her body, and the whispers in her mind seemed to quiet.

"Thank you," she said. "But what do I do next? How do I stop the Dark Covenant?"

Selene's expression grew serious. "The Dark Covenant is preparing for the Rite of Ascension," she said. "You must disrupt the ritual and break their hold on the village. But be warned—the path ahead will be perilous, and the choices you make will determine the fate of us all."

Sarah nodded, her resolve hardening. "I understand," she said. "I'll do whatever it takes to stop them."

Selene placed a hand on Sarah's shoulder, her eyes filled with a mixture of hope and sadness. "May the fates be with you, child," she said. "Remember, you are not alone. The villagers and those who believe in the prophecy will stand by your side."

With renewed determination, Sarah and Ethan left the cottage and made their way back to the village. The mark on Sarah's shoulder still pulsed with energy, but she felt more in control now, thanks to the amulet.

As they walked, Ethan turned to her, his expression serious. "Are you ready for this?" he asked. "The road ahead won't be easy."

Sarah nodded, her resolve unwavering. "I'm ready," she said. "We have to stop the Dark Covenant, no matter what it takes."

They spent the next few days preparing for the upcoming ritual. Sarah practiced focusing her newfound abilities with the help of the amulet, while Ethan gathered supplies and information from the villagers. They knew that disrupting the Rite of Ascension would be a dangerous and complex task, but they were determined to see it through.

The night of the ritual arrived, and Sarah and Ethan made their way to the stone circle. The air was thick with anticipation, and the forest seemed to come alive with shadows and whispers. They hid in the underbrush, watching as the members of the Covenant gathered around the circle, their torches casting an eerie glow.

The leader of the Covenant stepped forward, holding the ceremonial dagger aloft. He began to chant in a rhythmic pattern, his voice rising and falling with each incantation. The air around them seemed to vibrate with energy, and the torches flickered as though caught in an unseen wind.

Sarah and Ethan moved quickly, their hearts pounding with adrenaline. They knew that they had to act swiftly and decisively to disrupt the ritual and save the village.

As the chanting grew louder, Sarah felt the mark on her shoulder begin to burn with an intense heat. She focused on the amulet, drawing strength from its protective energy. She knew that she had to use her newfound abilities to disrupt the ritual and break the Covenant's hold on the village.

With a deep breath, Sarah stepped into the clearing, her eyes fixed on the leader of the Covenant. "Stop!" she shouted, her voice echoing through the night.

The chanting faltered, and the members of the Covenant turned to face her, their expressions hidden by their hoods. The leader's eyes widened in surprise, and for a moment, the air was filled with an eerie silence.

"You don't know what you're doing," Sarah said, her voice steady. "The Rite of Ascension will bring nothing but destruction."

The leader sneered, his grip on the dagger tightening. "You have no idea of the power we wield," he said. "The ritual must be completed. The prophecy demands it."

Sarah took a step forward, her resolve unwavering. "The prophecy also speaks of a chosen one who will save the village," she said. "And I intend to fulfill that role."

The leader's eyes narrowed, and he raised the dagger, preparing to complete the final incantation. But before he could bring the dagger down, Sarah focused her energy, channeling it through the amulet. A powerful wave of magic erupted from her, knocking the leader and the members of the Covenant to the ground.

The ground beneath the stone circle began to tremble, and a blinding light erupted from the center. The energy that had been building throughout the ritual was unleashed in a powerful wave, consuming the dark forces that had sought to control the village.

Sarah and Ethan took advantage of the chaos to rescue the sacrificial victim, a young woman who had been bound and gagged at the center of the circle. They untied her and helped her to her feet, urging her to run.

"Go!" Sarah shouted. "Get out of here and don't look back!"

The girl nodded, tears streaming down her face, and took off into the forest. Sarah and Ethan followed close behind, their hearts pounding with a mixture of fear and exhilaration.

When they finally reached the safety of the village, they didn't stop until they were inside the inn. The villagers had gathered outside, their expressions a mixture of fear and confusion.

"What happened?" one of them asked.

Sarah took a deep breath, her heart still racing. "We disrupted the ritual," she said. "The Dark Covenant's hold on this village is broken."

The villagers stared at her in disbelief, their expressions slowly transforming into relief and gratitude. The oppressive darkness that had hung over Raven's Hollow for so long began to lift, and the air seemed to grow lighter.

Over the next several days, Sarah and Ethan helped the villagers rebuild their lives. The members of the Covenant who had survived the disruption of the ritual were brought to justice, and the village began to heal.

Sarah knew that their journey was far from over. There were still many unanswered questions, and the threat of the Dark Covenant was not entirely gone. But for now, they had won a significant victory.

As the days turned into weeks and the weeks into months, Sarah and Ethan remained in Raven's Hollow, documenting the transformation and helping the villagers reclaim their lives. Their bond grew stronger, forged by the shared experiences and the challenges they had faced together.

In the end, Sarah had found more than just a story—she had found a purpose, a calling to uncover the truth and bring justice to those who needed it most. And with Ethan by her side, she knew they could face whatever challenges lay ahead.

The shadow mark on her shoulder was a constant reminder of the prophecy and the role she had been chosen to play. But it was also a symbol of her strength and resilience. With the amulet's protection and the support of her newfound allies, Sarah was ready to face whatever the future held.

The village of Raven's Hollow had begun to heal, and a new era of hope and resilience had dawned. As Sarah looked out over the village from the window of her room at the inn, she felt a sense of peace and fulfillment. The journey had been long and difficult, but it had also been worth it. She had found the story she had been searching for, and in the process, she had found herself.

The road ahead would undoubtedly bring new challenges and adventures, but Sarah was ready to face them head-on. With Ethan by her side and the support of the villagers, she knew that they could overcome any obstacle.

The shadow mark had opened her eyes to a world of ancient secrets and dark powers, but it had also shown her the strength of the human spirit and the power of resilience. As she closed the book she had been reading and looked out at the rising sun, she knew that the journey was only just beginning.

And with that thought, she turned to face the future with hope and determination, ready to uncover the truth and bring light to the darkest corners of the world.

Chapter 6: The Blood Moon

The rare blood moon, a celestial event that occurred once every few decades, was approaching, and the village of Raven's Hollow was buzzing with a mix of anticipation and unease. This phenomenon, where the moon takes on a reddish hue due to Earth's shadow, was steeped in local folklore and was said to hold great significance for the Dark Covenant. Sarah and Ethan knew that they had to act quickly to gather evidence that could expose the society and disrupt their plans.

The morning of the blood moon, the air was thick with tension. The villagers went about their daily routines with a nervous energy, their eyes frequently darting to the sky as if expecting it to turn red at any moment. The knowledge that the Dark Covenant was planning something significant weighed heavily on everyone, and whispers of dark rituals and sacrifices filled the air.

Sarah and Ethan were determined to uncover the Covenant's plans and put a stop to them. They spent the day gathering information from the villagers, piecing together the puzzle of the Dark Covenant's intentions. The clues led them to believe that the Covenant would use the blood moon's energy to perform a powerful ritual, one that could strengthen their hold on the village or even extend their influence beyond its borders.

As the sun began to set, casting long shadows across the village, Sarah and Ethan met in a secluded spot near the edge of the forest to discuss their plan.

"We need to find out where the ritual is taking place," Sarah said, her voice filled with urgency. "If we can gather evidence and document what they're doing, we can expose them and bring an end to this once and for all."

Ethan nodded, his expression serious. "Agreed. I've heard whispers of an underground chamber somewhere in the forest, a place where the Covenant performs their most secretive and powerful rituals. If we can find it, we might be able to stop them."

Sarah's heart raced at the thought. "Do you have any idea where this chamber might be?" she asked.

"I've heard rumors," Ethan replied. "There's an old, abandoned well deep in the forest. Some say it's a hidden entrance to the chamber. It's a long shot, but it's the best lead we have."

With the blood moon rising higher in the sky, casting an eerie red glow over the landscape, Sarah and Ethan set off into the forest. The path was dark and treacherous, and the shadows seemed to move of their own accord, but they pressed on, driven by a determination to uncover the truth and protect the village.

As they walked, the air grew colder, and the sounds of the forest seemed to fade away, leaving only an oppressive silence. Sarah couldn't shake the feeling that they were being watched, but she pushed the fear aside, focusing on the task at hand.

After what felt like hours of navigating the dense underbrush, they finally came upon the old well. It was overgrown with ivy and surrounded by a crumbling stone wall. The well's opening was covered by a rusty, iron grate, and the air around it felt thick with an unseen energy.

"This must be it," Ethan said, his voice barely above a whisper.

Sarah nodded, her heart pounding in her chest. "Let's see if we can get this grate off," she said.

They worked together to pry the grate loose, the rusty metal groaning in protest. After several minutes of struggle, they managed to lift it away, revealing a dark, narrow shaft leading down into the earth. The air that rose from the well was damp and musty, carrying with it a faint, metallic scent that made Sarah's stomach turn.

Ethan pulled out a flashlight and shone it down the shaft. The light revealed a series of worn, stone steps leading into the darkness. "I'll go first," he said. "Stay close behind me."

Sarah nodded, feeling a mixture of fear and determination. She followed Ethan down the steps, the darkness closing in around them as they descended. The walls of the shaft were damp and slick, and the air grew colder with each step they took.

After what felt like an eternity, they reached the bottom of the shaft and found themselves in a narrow, stone corridor. The air was thick with an oppressive energy, and the walls were lined with strange, glowing symbols that pulsed with an eerie light.

"This is it," Ethan said, his voice tense. "We're close."

They moved cautiously down the corridor, the light from Ethan's flashlight casting long shadows on the walls. The symbols seemed to writhe and twist as they passed, and Sarah couldn't shake the feeling that they were being watched.

As they turned a corner, they came upon a large, wooden door. The door was adorned with intricate carvings and strange symbols, and it radiated a powerful energy that made Sarah's skin crawl.

"This must be the entrance to the chamber," Ethan said. "We need to be careful. There's no telling what we'll find on the other side."

Sarah nodded, her heart racing. She took a deep breath and pushed the door open, revealing a large, underground chamber. The chamber was dimly lit by torches mounted on the walls, and the air was thick with the scent of incense and burning herbs.

In the center of the chamber stood a large, stone altar, covered with dark, crimson stains. Surrounding the altar were members of the Dark Covenant, their faces hidden by hooded cloaks. The leader of the Covenant stood at the head of the altar, holding a ceremonial dagger aloft. His voice echoed through the chamber as he chanted in a strange, rhythmic language.

Sarah and Ethan ducked behind a large, stone pillar, watching the ritual unfold. The leader of the Covenant raised the dagger higher, and the chanting grew louder, reverberating through the chamber. The torches flickered, and the air seemed to vibrate with energy.

"We need to document this," Sarah whispered, pulling out her camera. "We need evidence to expose them."

Ethan nodded and pulled out a small, handheld video camera. They began to record the ritual, capturing the chanting, the symbols on the walls, and the dark energy that filled the chamber.

As they watched, the leader of the Covenant lowered the dagger, pointing it at a figure bound to the altar. Sarah's heart skipped a beat as she realized that the figure was a young woman, her eyes wide with fear.

"We have to do something," Sarah whispered urgently. "We can't let them hurt her."

Ethan's expression was grim. "We need to find a way to disrupt the ritual," he said. "If we can break their focus, we might be able to save her."

Sarah's mind raced as she looked around the chamber, searching for something they could use. Her eyes fell on a large, ornate mirror mounted on the wall. The mirror was covered in strange symbols, and it seemed to pulse with a dark energy.

"That mirror," she said, pointing. "It looks important. Maybe if we break it, we can disrupt the ritual."

Ethan nodded, his eyes narrowing in determination. "It's worth a shot," he said. "Cover me while I get to it."

Sarah nodded, her heart pounding with fear and adrenaline. She watched as Ethan moved stealthily through the shadows, making his way towards the mirror. The chanting grew louder, and the energy in the chamber seemed to reach a fever pitch.

As Ethan approached the mirror, Sarah held her breath, praying that he wouldn't be seen. Just as he reached the mirror, the leader of the Covenant raised the dagger, preparing to bring it down on the bound woman.

Ethan swung the hilt of his knife at the mirror with all his strength, shattering the glass with a deafening crash. The chamber was suddenly filled with a blinding light, and the chanting faltered as the members of the Covenant cried out in shock.

The leader of the Covenant turned, his eyes blazing with fury. "Stop them!" he shouted.

Sarah and Ethan sprang into action, rushing to the altar to free the bound woman. The members of the Covenant moved to intercept them, but the disruption of the ritual had weakened their focus, and they stumbled, disoriented.

Sarah reached the altar and quickly untied the woman's bindings. "You're safe now," she said, helping her to her feet. "We need to get out of here."

The woman nodded, tears streaming down her face. Together, they ran towards the exit, Ethan close behind them. The members of the Covenant gave chase, but their movements were sluggish and uncoordinated, the disruption of the ritual leaving them weakened and confused.

As they reached the corridor, Sarah glanced back to see the leader of the Covenant standing at the altar, his face contorted with rage. "This isn't over," he shouted. "You can't stop us!"

Sarah turned and ran, the echoes of his words ringing in her ears. They made their way back up the shaft, the sounds of pursuit growing fainter with each step. When they finally emerged into the forest, they didn't stop until they were far from the well, the safety of the village in sight.

The villagers were waiting for them, their expressions a mixture of fear and hope. Sarah and Ethan explained what had happened, showing them the recordings and photographs they had taken as evidence. The villagers listened in stunned silence, their disbelief slowly giving way to anger and determination.

"We can't let the Dark Covenant continue their reign of terror," one of the villagers said. "We need to stand together and put an end to this."

The others nodded in agreement, their resolve strengthening. With the evidence Sarah and Ethan had gathered, they were able to expose the dark rituals and practices of the Covenant. The authorities were called in, and the members of the Covenant who had survived the disruption of the ritual were arrested and brought to justice.

Over the next few weeks, the village of Raven's Hollow began to heal. The oppressive darkness that had hung over the village for so long lifted, and the air seemed to grow lighter. The villagers, free from the fear and control of the Dark Covenant, began to rebuild their lives and their community.

Sarah and Ethan remained in the village, helping with the recovery and documenting the transformation. Their bond grew stronger, forged by the shared experiences and the challenges they had faced together.

In the end, Sarah had found more than just a story—she had found a purpose, a calling to uncover the truth and bring justice to those who needed it most. And with Ethan by her side, she knew they could face whatever challenges lay ahead.

The blood moon had been a turning point for the village of Raven's Hollow, a catalyst for change and a new beginning. As Sarah looked out over the village from the window of her room at the inn, she felt a sense of peace and fulfillment. The journey had been long and difficult, but it had also been worth it. She had found the story she had been searching for, and in the process, she had found herself.

The road ahead would undoubtedly bring new challenges and adventures, but Sarah was ready to face them head-on. With Ethan by her side and the support of the villagers, she knew that they could overcome any obstacle.

The blood moon had marked the end of the Dark Covenant's reign, but it had also marked the beginning of a new era of hope and resilience for Raven's Hollow. As she closed the book she had been reading and looked out at the rising sun, she knew that the journey was only just beginning.

And with that thought, she turned to face the future with hope and determination, ready to uncover the truth and bring light to the darkest corners of the world.

Chapter 7: The Betrayal

The village of Raven's Hollow was slowly returning to normalcy. With the Dark Covenant exposed and its members arrested, the oppressive atmosphere that had suffocated the village for so long began to lift. The villagers went about their daily lives with a newfound sense of freedom, and hope was beginning to bloom once more.

Sarah and Ethan had played a pivotal role in bringing about this change. Together, they had uncovered the dark secrets of the Covenant and disrupted their nefarious plans. But as the days passed, Sarah couldn't shake a growing sense of unease. There were too many unanswered questions, and Ethan's behavior had become increasingly erratic.

It started with small things—Ethan disappearing for hours without explanation, his cryptic responses when she asked where he had been, and the way he avoided her gaze when she pressed him for answers. Sarah tried to convince herself that it was just the stress of recent events, but the nagging doubt gnawed at her.

One night, as she lay in bed, sleep eluding her, she heard Ethan leave the inn. The clock on her nightstand read 2:00 AM. Curiosity and suspicion overcame her, and she quietly got out of bed, throwing on a jacket. She followed Ethan at a safe distance, making sure to stay hidden in the shadows.

Ethan walked purposefully through the village, his movements deliberate and cautious. He headed toward the edge of the forest, where the trees loomed like silent sentinels in the moonlight. Sarah's heart pounded in her chest as she followed him deeper into the woods.

After what felt like an eternity, they arrived at a small, secluded clearing. Ethan stopped and looked around, as if ensuring he wasn't being followed. Sarah ducked behind a tree, her breath coming in shallow gasps. She watched as Ethan pulled out a small, leather-bound book and began to chant in a low, rhythmic voice.

The air around him seemed to shimmer with an otherworldly energy, and Sarah's blood ran cold. She recognized the symbols and the cadence of the chant—it was the same dark magic used by the Dark Covenant.

Her mind raced with confusion and betrayal. How could Ethan, the man who had fought alongside her to expose the Covenant, be using their dark magic? Was he secretly a member of the Covenant all along, or had he been corrupted by their power?

Unable to remain silent any longer, Sarah stepped into the clearing, her voice trembling with anger and hurt. "Ethan, what are you doing?"

Ethan froze, his eyes wide with shock and guilt. He quickly closed the book and turned to face her. "Sarah, it's not what it looks like," he said, his voice pleading.

"Then what is it?" Sarah demanded. "Explain to me why you're performing a dark ritual in the middle of the night."

Ethan took a deep breath, his shoulders slumping. "I didn't want you to find out this way," he said. "But you deserve the truth."

Sarah crossed her arms, her gaze unwavering. "Start talking."

Ethan hesitated for a moment before speaking. "I was a member of the Dark Covenant," he admitted. "But I left them long before you came to Raven's Hollow. I realized the darkness they wielded was too dangerous, and I couldn't be a part of it anymore."

Sarah's mind reeled. "Why didn't you tell me?" she asked. "Why keep it a secret?"

"Because I was afraid," Ethan said. "Afraid that you wouldn't trust me, that you would see me as one of them. But I swear, Sarah, I left them because I wanted to fight against their darkness, not embrace it."

Sarah's heart ached with a mix of anger and sorrow. "And the ritual you were performing just now? What was that about?"

Ethan looked down at the book in his hands. "I've been trying to find a way to protect us, to keep the dark forces at bay," he said. "The rituals I learned as a member of the Covenant can be used for good, too. I was trying to create a protective barrier around the village."

Sarah wanted to believe him, but the doubts lingered. "Why didn't you tell me? We could have worked together."

"I didn't want to burden you with my past," Ethan said. "And I didn't want to risk you getting hurt because of me. But I see now that keeping secrets was a mistake."

Sarah's anger flared. "Damn right it was a mistake. Do you have any idea how much trust we've built? How much we've gone through together? And you kept this from me?"

Ethan's eyes filled with regret. "I know, and I'm sorry. I should have told you everything from the beginning. I just... I didn't want to lose you."

Sarah's resolve wavered, but the hurt was too deep. "I need time to think," she said, turning away from him. "I can't deal with this right now."

Ethan reached out, his hand brushing her arm. "Sarah, please. Let me make it right."

Sarah pulled away, her eyes filled with tears. "I don't know if you can," she said softly. "I need some time alone."

With that, she turned and walked back through the forest, leaving Ethan standing in the clearing, his heart heavy with regret.

Sarah returned to the inn, her mind a whirlwind of emotions. She felt betrayed, hurt, and confused. She had trusted Ethan, relied on him, and now everything seemed uncertain. She knew she couldn't stay in Raven's Hollow, at least not for the time being. She needed to clear her head and figure out what to do next.

The next morning, Sarah packed her bags and left a note for Ethan. She didn't say where she was going, only that she needed some time alone. She slipped out of the inn and made her way to the bus station, determined to put some distance between herself and the village.

As the bus pulled away from Raven's Hollow, Sarah stared out the window, her heart heavy with sorrow. She didn't know where she was going or what she would do next, but she knew she couldn't stay in the village with the shadow of betrayal hanging over her.

The bus ride was long and uneventful, giving Sarah plenty of time to think. She replayed the events of the past few weeks over and over in her mind, trying to make sense of everything. She couldn't shake the feeling that there was more to Ethan's story than he had told her, but she didn't know how to find out the truth.

She arrived in a small town several hours away and checked into a motel. The room was small and sparsely furnished, but it was a place to rest and think. She spent the next few days in a state of limbo, trying to come to terms with her feelings and figure out what to do next.

One evening, as she sat on the bed, staring at the ceiling, her phone rang. It was a number she didn't recognize, but she answered it anyway.

"Hello?"

"Sarah, it's Ethan."

Sarah's heart skipped a beat. "Ethan, what do you want?"

"I know you need time, but there's something you need to know," Ethan said, his voice filled with urgency. "I've been doing more research, and I've uncovered something important about the Dark Covenant. Something that could change everything."

Sarah's curiosity was piqued, despite her lingering anger. "What is it?"

"The Covenant's plans go deeper than we thought," Ethan said. "They're not just trying to control Raven's Hollow. They're trying to tap into an ancient power that could have catastrophic consequences for the entire region. I need your help to stop them."

Sarah took a deep breath, her mind racing. "Why should I trust you?" she asked. "After everything you've kept from me, how do I know you're not just using me?"

Ethan's voice was filled with sincerity. "I understand your hesitation, but I swear I'm telling you the truth. I want to make things right, and I need your help to do it. Please, Sarah, give me a chance to prove myself."

Sarah's resolve wavered. She wanted to believe him, but the pain of his betrayal was still fresh. "I'll think about it," she said finally. "But no promises."

"That's all I can ask," Ethan said. "Thank you, Sarah. I'll be in touch."

Sarah hung up the phone, her emotions in turmoil. She didn't know what to do, but she couldn't ignore the possibility that Ethan was telling the truth. If the Dark Covenant's plans were as dangerous as he said, she couldn't just walk away.

Over the next few days, Sarah wrestled with her decision. She wanted to trust Ethan, but the betrayal still stung. She spent hours poring over her notes and the evidence they had gathered, trying to piece together the puzzle of the Dark Covenant's plans.

One night, as she lay in bed, a realization struck her. She couldn't let her personal feelings cloud her judgment. If there was even a chance that Ethan was telling the truth, she had to act. The stakes were too high to let her emotions get in the way.

With renewed determination, Sarah packed her bags and left the motel. She took the first bus back to Raven's Hollow, her mind focused on the task ahead. She didn't know what awaited her, but she knew she had to face it head-on.

When she arrived in the village, the atmosphere was tense. The villagers were on edge, and there was a palpable sense of fear in the air. Sarah made her way to the inn, where Ethan was waiting for her.

"Sarah," he said, relief evident in his eyes. "Thank you for coming back."

Sarah nodded, her expression serious. "Let's get to work," she said. "Tell me everything you've found."

Ethan led her to a secluded spot in the forest, away from prying eyes. He spread out a map and a series of documents, explaining what he had uncovered.

"The Dark Covenant is trying to harness the power of an ancient artifact," he said. "It's called the Stone of Shadows, and it has the ability to amplify dark magic. If they succeed, they could unleash a wave of destruction that would be catastrophic."

Sarah's heart raced as she listened. "Where is this artifact?" she asked.

"It's hidden in an underground chamber beneath the old church," Ethan said. "We need to get there before they do and destroy it."

Sarah nodded, her determination renewed. "Let's go."

They made their way to the old church, moving cautiously through the shadows. The church was a dilapidated structure, its windows shattered and its walls covered in ivy. Ethan led the way to a hidden entrance at the back of the building, a narrow staircase leading down into the darkness.

As they descended, the air grew colder, and the oppressive energy of the underground chamber pressed in around them. They moved silently, their footsteps echoing off the stone walls.

When they reached the bottom of the staircase, they found themselves in a large, dimly lit chamber. The walls were lined with strange, glowing symbols, and in the center of the room stood a large, stone pedestal. Atop the pedestal rested a dark, crystalline stone that pulsed with a malevolent energy.

"This is it," Ethan said, his voice tense. "The Stone of Shadows."

Sarah's eyes were drawn to the stone, its dark energy calling to her. She felt a strange compulsion to reach out and touch it, but she resisted, knowing the danger it posed.

"We need to destroy it," she said, her voice firm. "How do we do that?"

Ethan pulled out a small, silver amulet. "This amulet has the power to neutralize dark magic," he said. "We need to place it on the stone and recite the incantation written in this book."

He handed Sarah a worn, leather-bound book filled with ancient symbols and incantations. She took a deep breath and nodded. "Let's do this."

They moved to the pedestal, and Ethan placed the amulet on the stone. Sarah opened the book and began to read the incantation, her voice steady and clear. The air around them seemed to vibrate with energy, and the symbols on the walls pulsed with a rhythmic light.

As she recited the incantation, the dark energy of the stone began to wane, its malevolent glow dimming. But just as they neared the end of the incantation, a group of figures emerged from the shadows, their eyes filled with fury.

The leader of the Dark Covenant stepped forward, his voice filled with venom. "You dare to interfere with our plans?"

Sarah and Ethan turned to face them, their resolve unwavering. "We won't let you unleash this darkness," Sarah said, her voice firm.

A tense standoff ensued, the air thick with anticipation. The members of the Covenant moved to attack, but Sarah and Ethan were ready. They fought with a determination born of necessity, their movements swift and precise.

In the midst of the battle, Sarah saw an opening and moved to complete the incantation. She spoke the final words, and the amulet glowed with a brilliant light. The Stone of Shadows cracked and shattered, its dark energy dissipating into the air.

The members of the Covenant cried out in anguish as their power was broken. The chamber shook with a violent tremor, and the symbols on the walls flickered and went dark.

Sarah and Ethan stood together, their breaths coming in heavy gasps. The chamber was silent, the oppressive energy lifted. They had succeeded in their mission, but the cost had been high.

As they made their way back to the village, Sarah felt a sense of closure. The Dark Covenant had been defeated, and the threat of the Stone of Shadows had been neutralized. But the betrayal and secrets that had come to light still weighed heavily on her heart.

When they reached the inn, Sarah turned to Ethan, her expression somber. "We did it," she said. "But things will never be the same between us."

Ethan's eyes filled with regret. "I know," he said. "And I'm sorry for everything. I hope that one day, you'll be able to forgive me."

Sarah nodded, her heart heavy with the weight of their shared history. "Maybe," she said. "But for now, I need some time."

Ethan nodded, understanding. "Take all the time you need," he said. "I'll be here if you ever need me."

Sarah watched as he walked away, her emotions in turmoil. She didn't know what the future held, but she knew that she had to move forward, one step at a time.

Over the next few days, Sarah focused on helping the villagers rebuild their lives. She documented their stories and worked to ensure that the truth of the Dark Covenant's reign was known. The village began to heal, its people finding strength in each other and in the promise of a brighter future.

As the weeks turned into months, Sarah found a sense of peace and purpose. She had uncovered the truth, faced the darkness, and come out stronger on the other side. The journey had been long and difficult, but it had also been worth it.

The road ahead would undoubtedly bring new challenges and adventures, but Sarah was ready to face them head-on. With the support of the villagers and the knowledge she had gained, she knew that she could overcome any obstacle.

The betrayal had left its mark, but it had also taught her valuable lessons about trust, resilience, and the power of the human spirit. As she looked out over the village from the window of her room at the inn, she felt a sense of peace and fulfillment.

The journey was only just beginning, and Sarah was ready to embrace it with hope and determination. She had found the story she had been searching for, and in the process, she had found herself. And with that thought, she turned to face the future, ready to uncover the truth and bring light to the darkest corners of the world.

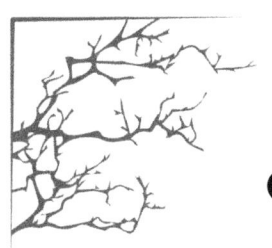

Chapter 8: The Lost Manuscript

The morning sun filtered through the curtains of Sarah's room at the inn, casting a warm glow that contrasted sharply with the tumultuous thoughts swirling in her mind. The past few months had been a whirlwind of revelations and betrayals, but also of small victories against the dark forces that had held Raven's Hollow in their grip for so long. Despite the progress, Sarah knew their work was far from over. The Dark Covenant's influence, though weakened, still loomed ominously.

Determined to find a permanent solution, Sarah spent her days poring over ancient texts and interviewing villagers who had lived through the Covenant's reign. One morning, as she was organizing her notes, she received a knock on her door. It was Mrs. Hawthorne, an elderly villager who had lived in Raven's Hollow her entire life.

"Good morning, Sarah," Mrs. Hawthorne greeted, her voice tinged with urgency. "There's something you need to see."

Intrigued, Sarah followed Mrs. Hawthorne through the village to an old, dilapidated house on the outskirts. The house had clearly been abandoned for years, its windows boarded up and the paint peeling from the walls.

"This was the home of Thomas Blackwood," Mrs. Hawthorne explained. "He was a member of the Dark Covenant, but he tried to escape. Before he disappeared, he left behind a manuscript. It details everything he knew about the Covenant and how to destroy it."

Sarah's heart quickened with anticipation. This could be the breakthrough they needed. Together, they entered the house, the air thick with dust and the scent of decay. Mrs. Hawthorne led her to a small, hidden room at the back of the house. Inside, they found an old desk, covered in a thick layer of dust. On the desk lay a leather-bound manuscript, its pages yellowed with age.

Sarah carefully picked up the manuscript, her fingers trembling with excitement. "Thank you, Mrs. Hawthorne," she said, her voice filled with gratitude. "This could be exactly what we need."

Mrs. Hawthorne nodded. "I hope it helps," she said. "Good luck, Sarah."

Back at the inn, Sarah eagerly began to read the manuscript. It was written in a mixture of English and Latin, the handwriting meticulous and filled with intricate symbols. The manuscript was a detailed account of Thomas Blackwood's time in the Dark Covenant, his growing disillusionment, and his desperate attempts to escape.

As Sarah delved deeper into the manuscript, she uncovered a wealth of information about the Covenant's rituals and the dark magic they wielded. But what intrigued her most was the section detailing how to destroy the Covenant. Thomas had meticulously documented a series of rituals that, if performed correctly, could break the Covenant's hold on Raven's Hollow and neutralize their dark powers once and for all.

Sarah's excitement grew as she deciphered the rituals. The key to breaking the curse lay in a combination of ancient incantations and specific actions that had to be performed at precise times. The blood moon had been a crucial element in the Covenant's power, but there were other celestial events that could be used to counteract their magic.

One of the most significant rituals involved an artifact called the Eye of Anubis, a powerful talisman that had been used by the Covenant to channel their dark magic. According to Thomas, the Eye of Anubis had to be destroyed in a specific manner to sever the Covenant's connection to the other realm.

Sarah knew she couldn't do this alone. She needed Ethan's help, despite the lingering tension between them. She found him in the village square, helping the villagers repair a damaged building.

"Ethan," she called, her voice steady but urgent. "I need to talk to you."

Ethan looked up, his expression wary but curious. "What is it, Sarah?"

"I've found a manuscript," she said, holding up the leather-bound book. "It was written by Thomas Blackwood, a former member of the Covenant. It details how to destroy the Covenant once and for all."

Ethan's eyes widened with interest. "That's incredible. What does it say?"

Sarah quickly explained the key points of the manuscript, emphasizing the importance of the Eye of Anubis and the specific rituals needed to break the curse.

Ethan listened intently, his expression growing more serious. "We need to find the Eye of Anubis," he said. "If we can destroy it, we can sever the Covenant's power for good."

Sarah nodded. "But we have to be careful. The manuscript also warns of the dangers of performing these rituals. We need to make sure we get everything right."

Over the next few days, Sarah and Ethan worked tirelessly to decipher the manuscript and gather the necessary materials for the rituals. They enlisted the help of the villagers, who were eager to do whatever they could to rid their home of the Covenant's influence once and for all.

The first step was to locate the Eye of Anubis. According to the manuscript, the artifact had been hidden in a secret chamber beneath the old church, the same place where they had disrupted the Covenant's last ritual. Sarah and Ethan prepared to venture back into the underground chamber, this time with a clear purpose and a detailed plan.

As they descended the narrow staircase, the air grew colder, and the oppressive energy of the chamber pressed in around them. They moved cautiously, their flashlights casting eerie shadows on the stone walls.

When they reached the chamber, they found it much as they had left it. The Stone of Shadows lay shattered on the ground, its dark energy dissipated. But there was no sign of the Eye of Anubis.

"We need to find a hidden compartment," Sarah said, recalling Thomas's description in the manuscript. "It's supposed to be behind one of these walls."

They carefully examined the walls, searching for any sign of a hidden entrance. After several minutes of searching, Sarah noticed a faint outline of a rectangular panel in one of the walls. She pressed on the panel, and it shifted slightly, revealing a small, hidden alcove.

Inside the alcove lay a small, ornate box. Sarah carefully removed the box and opened it, revealing a dark, crystalline talisman—the Eye of Anubis. The talisman seemed to pulse with a malevolent energy, and Sarah felt a chill run down her spine as she held it.

"We have it," she said, her voice trembling with a mix of excitement and apprehension. "Now we just need to destroy it."

According to the manuscript, the Eye of Anubis could only be destroyed during a specific celestial alignment. The alignment was set to occur in just a few days, giving them little time to prepare. They returned to the village and gathered the necessary materials for the ritual, enlisting the help of Selene, the local witch, who had a deep understanding of the ancient magic they were dealing with.

As the day of the celestial alignment approached, the tension in the village grew palpable. The villagers were nervous but determined, their resolve strengthened by the promise of finally being free from the Covenant's influence.

On the night of the alignment, Sarah, Ethan, and Selene gathered in the village square, surrounded by the villagers who had come to witness the ritual. The sky was clear, and the stars shone brightly overhead. The air was charged with an electric energy, and Sarah felt a sense of both fear and anticipation.

Selene took her place at the center of the square, the Eye of Anubis resting on a stone pedestal before her. She began to chant in a low, rhythmic voice, calling upon the ancient magic to aid them in their task.

Sarah and Ethan stood beside her, holding the materials needed for the ritual. As Selene's chant grew louder, the air around them seemed to vibrate with energy, and the symbols carved into the pedestal began to glow with a bright, white light.

"Now," Selene said, her voice steady. "Place the amulet on the talisman and recite the incantation."

Sarah took a deep breath and placed the silver amulet on the Eye of Anubis. She opened the manuscript and began to recite the incantation, her voice clear and unwavering. The words felt powerful and ancient, resonating deep within her soul.

As she spoke, the Eye of Anubis began to pulse with a dark, malevolent energy. The air around them crackled with electricity, and the ground beneath their feet trembled. Sarah could feel the power of the talisman resisting their efforts, but she pressed on, determined to see the ritual through.

Ethan joined in the incantation, his voice blending with Sarah's. The energy in the square intensified, and the symbols on the pedestal glowed even brighter.

The villagers watched in awe and fear, their hope hanging on the success of the ritual.

Suddenly, a powerful wave of dark energy erupted from the Eye of Anubis, knocking Sarah, Ethan, and Selene to the ground. The talisman pulsed violently, its dark energy struggling against the power of the incantation.

"Keep going!" Selene urged, her voice strained. "We can't stop now!"

Sarah and Ethan scrambled to their feet and resumed the incantation, their voices rising above the roar of the dark energy. The Eye of Anubis glowed brighter and brighter, its malevolent power reaching a fever pitch.

Just as it seemed the talisman might overpower them, the celestial alignment reached its peak. A brilliant beam of light descended from the sky, striking the Eye of Anubis and enveloping it in a blinding radiance.

The dark energy of the talisman began to wane, its power being consumed by the light. Sarah and Ethan continued the incantation, their voices unwavering. The Eye of Anubis cracked and splintered, its dark energy dissipating into the air.

With one final burst of light, the Eye of Anubis shattered into a thousand pieces, its malevolent power destroyed. The ground beneath their feet steadied, and the air grew calm and still.

The villagers erupted into cheers, their faces alight with joy and relief. The oppressive darkness that had hung over Raven's Hollow for so long was finally lifted. The Dark Covenant's power was broken, and the village was free.

Sarah and Ethan stood together, their hearts filled with a mixture of exhaustion and triumph. They had done it. They had destroyed the Eye of Anubis and severed the Covenant's hold on the village.

Over the next few days, the village of Raven's Hollow began to transform. The fear and tension that had gripped the villagers gave way to hope and resilience. They worked together to rebuild their community, drawing strength from each other and the promise of a brighter future.

Sarah and Ethan remained in the village, helping with the recovery and documenting the transformation. Their bond grew stronger, forged by the shared experiences and the challenges they had faced together.

In the end, Sarah had found more than just a story—she had found a purpose, a calling to uncover the truth and bring justice to those who needed it most. And with Ethan by her side, she knew they could face whatever challenges lay ahead.

The lost manuscript had been the key to their victory, a testament to the courage and determination of those who had fought against the darkness. As Sarah looked out over the village from the window of her room at the inn, she felt a sense of peace and fulfillment. The journey had been long and difficult, but it had also been worth it. She had found the story she had been searching for, and in the process, she had found herself.

The road ahead would undoubtedly bring new challenges and adventures, but Sarah was ready to face them head-on. With Ethan by her side and the support of the villagers, she knew that they could overcome any obstacle.

The lost manuscript had revealed the secrets of the Dark Covenant, but it had also shown Sarah the strength of the human spirit and the power of resilience. As she closed the book she had been reading and looked out at the rising sun, she knew that the journey was only just beginning.

And with that thought, she turned to face the future with hope and determination, ready to uncover the truth and bring light to the darkest corners of the world.

Chapter 9: The Witch's Curse

The village of Raven's Hollow had begun to rebuild itself, the oppressive shadow of the Dark Covenant lifting and giving way to an era of hope. Yet, despite the progress, Sarah felt a lingering sense of unease. The fight against the Covenant had revealed dark secrets and ancient powers that still simmered beneath the surface. She knew that the road to lasting peace was fraught with danger and uncertainty.

One evening, as Sarah walked through the village, she felt a strange compulsion to visit Selene, the local witch who had been instrumental in their recent victory. Selene's cottage lay on the outskirts of the village, nestled at the edge of the forest. The path was overgrown, and the air felt thick with an energy that both comforted and unnerved Sarah.

When she reached the cottage, she found Selene waiting for her at the door, as if she had anticipated her visit. Selene's piercing blue eyes were filled with a mixture of wisdom and sorrow, and her long silver hair flowed around her shoulders like a halo.

"Welcome, Sarah," Selene said, her voice soft but commanding. "I have been expecting you."

Sarah felt a shiver run down her spine. "You knew I was coming?"

Selene nodded. "There are things you need to know, things that only I can tell you."

Sarah followed Selene into the cottage, the familiar scent of herbs and incense filling the air. The interior was cluttered with jars, trinkets, and ancient books, each item seemingly imbued with a history of its own. They sat at a large wooden table in the center of the room, and Selene began to speak.

"I have been a part of this village for longer than you can imagine," Selene said, her eyes distant. "And I have a connection to the Dark Covenant that you must understand."

Sarah's heart skipped a beat. "What do you mean?"

Selene sighed, her expression pained. "I was once a member of the Dark Covenant," she admitted. "Many years ago, before you or even your parents were born. I was drawn to their promise of power and knowledge. But I soon realized the darkness they wielded was too great, and I left."

Sarah listened in stunned silence. "Why didn't you tell us this before?"

"Because I feared what you might think of me," Selene said. "And because I have been trying to atone for my past ever since I left the Covenant. I have dedicated my life to protecting this village and fighting against the darkness I once embraced."

Sarah felt a mix of anger and understanding. "And the rituals, the magic—how do you know so much?"

"Because I was once a part of it," Selene said. "I learned their secrets, their spells, their rituals. And I have used that knowledge to fight against them."

Selene reached into a drawer and pulled out a small, ornate amulet. It was intricately carved with symbols that glowed faintly in the dim light. "This amulet is a powerful protection charm," she said, handing it to Sarah. "It will shield you from the dark forces that seek to harm you. Wear it at all times."

Sarah took the amulet, feeling a strange warmth spread through her body as she held it. "Thank you," she said. "But why now? Why tell me this now?"

"Because there is something coming," Selene said, her voice grave. "A darkness greater than any we have faced before. The Dark Covenant may have been defeated, but their power lingers. And there are those who seek to revive it."

Sarah's heart pounded in her chest. "What do we do?"

"We prepare," Selene said. "We gather our strength, our knowledge, our allies. And we stand ready to face whatever comes."

Over the next few days, Sarah wore the amulet constantly, feeling its protective energy envelop her like a shield. She and Selene worked together to strengthen the village's defenses, using ancient spells and wards to create a barrier against the dark forces that threatened them.

One night, as they were preparing another protective spell, Selene suddenly stopped, her eyes narrowing in concentration. "Something is coming," she said, her voice tense. "I can feel it."

Sarah's heart raced as she followed Selene outside. The air was thick with an oppressive energy, and the night seemed darker than usual. They moved quickly through the village, alert for any sign of danger.

As they reached the edge of the forest, a group of shadowy figures emerged from the trees, their eyes glowing with a malevolent light. It was clear that these were remnants of the Dark Covenant, still determined to reclaim their power.

Selene stepped forward, her voice commanding. "Leave this place," she said. "You have no power here."

The leader of the group sneered, his voice dripping with contempt. "You cannot stop us, witch. We will reclaim what is rightfully ours."

Selene raised her hands, and a powerful wave of energy emanated from her, creating a barrier between them and the intruders. "You will not harm this village," she said, her voice unwavering.

The dark figures advanced, their malevolent energy pushing against Selene's barrier. Sarah could feel the intensity of the struggle, the air crackling with dark and light forces clashing.

As the leader of the intruders drew closer, he raised a hand and unleashed a powerful blast of dark energy. Selene's barrier wavered, and Sarah felt a surge of fear. She knew that Selene couldn't hold them off forever.

"Sarah, run!" Selene shouted, her voice strained with effort. "Get to safety!"

Sarah hesitated, her heart torn between the desire to stay and fight and the need to follow Selene's command. But as the dark energy continued to batter against the barrier, she knew she had no choice.

She turned and ran, her heart pounding in her chest. She could hear the sounds of the struggle behind her, Selene's voice chanting incantations as she fought to hold off the attackers.

As she reached the center of the village, she heard a cry of pain. She turned to see Selene fall to her knees, the dark energy overwhelming her. The leader of the intruders laughed, his voice filled with triumph.

"No!" Sarah screamed, her heart breaking. She started to run back towards Selene, but the witch raised a hand, her eyes filled with a mixture of determination and sorrow.

"Stay back, Sarah," Selene said, her voice weak but resolute. "This is my fight."

With a final, powerful incantation, Selene unleashed a wave of light that enveloped the dark figures. They screamed in agony as the light consumed them, their forms disintegrating into nothingness.

But the effort was too much for Selene. As the last of the intruders vanished, she collapsed to the ground, her energy spent. Sarah rushed to her side, tears streaming down her face.

"Selene, no," she whispered, her voice choked with emotion. "You can't leave us."

Selene reached up and touched Sarah's face, her eyes filled with a mix of pain and peace. "My time has come," she said softly. "But you are strong, Sarah. You will carry on the fight."

Sarah shook her head, her heart breaking. "I can't do this without you."

"You can," Selene said, her voice growing weaker. "And you must. The village needs you. The world needs you. Remember what I have taught you. Use the amulet. Protect the ones you love."

With those final words, Selene's eyes closed, and her body went still. Sarah cradled her in her arms, her heart shattered by the loss of the woman who had been both a mentor and a friend.

The villagers gathered around them, their faces filled with grief and gratitude. They knew the sacrifice Selene had made to protect them, and they vowed to honor her memory by continuing the fight against the darkness.

Over the next few days, Sarah threw herself into her work, determined to uphold Selene's legacy. She strengthened the protective wards around the village, using the knowledge Selene had imparted to her. She trained with the villagers, teaching them how to defend themselves and harness the power of the amulet.

The amulet became a symbol of hope and resilience for the village, its protective energy a constant reminder of Selene's sacrifice. Sarah wore it with pride, feeling its warmth and strength envelop her like a shield.

Despite the grief that weighed heavily on her heart, Sarah knew she couldn't afford to dwell on the past. The fight against the darkness was far from over, and she needed to stay vigilant. She spent countless hours researching ancient texts and deciphering the remaining secrets of the Dark Covenant, determined to uncover any hidden threats that might still lurk in the shadows.

One day, as Sarah was studying a particularly cryptic text, she came across a passage that mentioned a powerful artifact known as the Heart of Darkness. According to the text, the Heart of Darkness was a source of immense dark energy, capable of corrupting even the strongest of souls. It had been hidden away by the founders of the Dark Covenant, who had sought to harness its power for their own nefarious purposes.

Sarah knew that if the Heart of Darkness still existed, it posed a grave threat to the village and the surrounding region. She couldn't allow it to fall into the wrong hands. With the villagers' help, she began to search for any clues that might lead them to the artifact.

Their search led them to an ancient, overgrown temple deep within the forest. The temple was shrouded in darkness, its stone walls covered in moss and vines. The air inside was thick with a sense of foreboding, and Sarah could feel the presence of the dark energy that emanated from the Heart of Darkness.

As they explored the temple, they encountered a series of traps and obstacles, designed to protect the artifact from intruders. Sarah's heart raced as they navigated the treacherous path, her determination to protect the village driving her forward.

Finally, they reached the inner sanctum of the temple, a large chamber with a raised pedestal at its center. Atop the pedestal rested a dark, crystalline heart, pulsing with a malevolent energy. The Heart of Darkness.

Sarah approached the pedestal cautiously, feeling the dark energy wash over her like a wave. She knew that destroying the artifact would be no easy task, but she also knew that she couldn't allow it to remain intact.

As she reached for the Heart of Darkness, a shadowy figure emerged from the darkness, its eyes glowing with a sinister light. It was the spirit of one of the founders of the Dark Covenant, bound to the artifact and determined to protect it.

"You cannot destroy the Heart of Darkness," the spirit said, its voice echoing through the chamber. "Its power is eternal, and it will consume you."

Sarah felt a surge of fear, but she pushed it aside, focusing on the strength she had gained from Selene and the amulet. "I will not let the darkness win," she said, her voice steady.

With a deep breath, she raised the amulet and began to recite an incantation, drawing upon the ancient magic that Selene had taught her. The air around her crackled with energy, and the Heart of Darkness pulsed violently, its dark power struggling against the light.

The spirit of the founder screamed in rage and pain, its form writhing as the light from the amulet enveloped it. The chamber shook with the force of their struggle, the ancient stone walls groaning under the pressure.

But Sarah's resolve was unwavering. She continued the incantation, her voice growing stronger with each word. The light from the amulet intensified, and the Heart of Darkness began to crack and splinter, its dark energy dissipating into the air.

With a final burst of light, the Heart of Darkness shattered into a thousand pieces, its malevolent power destroyed. The spirit of the founder let out one last anguished cry before vanishing into nothingness.

The chamber grew still, the oppressive darkness lifting to reveal a sense of peace and tranquility. Sarah stood in the center of the room, her heart filled with a mixture of exhaustion and triumph. She had done it. She had destroyed the Heart of Darkness and severed its connection to the Dark Covenant.

As she made her way back to the village, she couldn't help but feel a sense of closure. The fight against the darkness had been long and arduous, but they had prevailed. Selene's sacrifice had not been in vain, and the village was finally free from the threat of the Dark Covenant.

The villagers greeted her with cheers and tears of joy, their faces alight with gratitude and relief. They knew that the darkness had been defeated, and they vowed to honor the memory of Selene and all those who had fought to protect them.

Over the next few weeks, the village of Raven's Hollow continued to rebuild and heal. The sense of community and resilience that had been forged in the face of adversity grew stronger with each passing day. Sarah continued to work alongside the villagers, using her knowledge and skills to help them create a brighter future.

The amulet, once a symbol of protection and hope, became a cherished heirloom, passed down through generations as a reminder of the strength and courage that had saved the village. Sarah wore it with pride, feeling its warmth and strength envelop her like a shield.

Despite the challenges they had faced, Sarah knew that the fight against the darkness had made them stronger. They had learned the value of unity, resilience, and the power of the human spirit. And as they looked to the future, they did so with hope and determination, ready to face whatever challenges lay ahead.

The journey had been long and difficult, but it had also been worth it. Sarah had found the story she had been searching for, and in the process, she had found herself. As she looked out over the village from the window of her room at the inn, she felt a sense of peace and fulfillment. The road ahead would undoubtedly bring new adventures, but she was ready to face them head-on.

And with that thought, she turned to face the future with hope and determination, ready to uncover the truth and bring light to the darkest corners of the world.

Chapter 10: The Infernal Gate

The village of Raven's Hollow had experienced a period of relative peace since the defeat of the Dark Covenant and the destruction of the Heart of Darkness. The villagers were rebuilding their lives, and a sense of normalcy was beginning to return. However, Sarah remained vigilant. She knew that the darkness that had plagued the village for so long might not be entirely vanquished.

One morning, as she was going through some of the old texts and manuscripts she had collected, Sarah came across a reference to something called the "Infernal Gate." The text was cryptic, but it suggested that the gate was a portal to the underworld, controlled by the Dark Covenant. The passage hinted that closing the Infernal Gate was crucial to breaking the Covenant's power once and for all.

Sarah's heart raced as she read the passage. The thought of a portal to the underworld being hidden somewhere in or around the village was both terrifying and fascinating. She knew that she needed to learn more about the Infernal Gate and how to close it.

Determined to uncover the truth, Sarah sought out Selene's old journals, hoping that the witch had left behind some information about the gate. She found the journals hidden away in a chest in Selene's cottage. As she pored over the pages, she discovered detailed accounts of Selene's time in the Dark Covenant and her subsequent efforts to protect the village. One entry, in particular, stood out:

"The Infernal Gate is the source of the Covenant's power. It is a portal to the underworld, through which they draw their dark energy. To break their hold on Raven's Hollow, the gate must be closed. The key to the gate lies in the ancient runes, which can only be deciphered by one who possesses the Eye of Anubis. The gate is hidden deep within the forest, protected by powerful wards."

Sarah felt a chill run down her spine as she read the entry. The Eye of Anubis had been destroyed, but she remembered the silver amulet Selene had given her. Perhaps it held the power to decipher the runes and close the gate.

She knew she couldn't do this alone. She needed Ethan's help. Despite the lingering tension between them, she trusted him and knew that he was committed to protecting the village. She found him in the village square, talking with some of the villagers.

"Ethan," she called, her voice urgent. "We need to talk."

Ethan looked up, his expression serious. "What is it, Sarah?"

"I found something," she said, holding up Selene's journal. "It's about the Infernal Gate—a portal to the underworld controlled by the Covenant. We need to close it to break their power once and for all."

Ethan's eyes widened with concern. "A portal to the underworld? Are you sure?"

Sarah nodded. "Yes. Selene wrote about it in her journal. The gate is hidden deep within the forest, and the key to closing it lies in ancient runes that can only be deciphered with the Eye of Anubis."

"But the Eye of Anubis was destroyed," Ethan said.

"I know," Sarah replied. "But I think the amulet Selene gave me might be able to help. We need to find the gate and close it before it's too late."

Ethan took a deep breath, his resolve firm. "Then let's find it."

Sarah and Ethan spent the next few days preparing for their journey into the forest. They gathered supplies, reviewed maps, and consulted with the villagers who had knowledge of the forest's hidden paths. They knew that the journey would be dangerous, but they were determined to succeed.

On the morning of their departure, the villagers gathered to see them off. There was a sense of apprehension in the air, but also a quiet determination. The villagers knew that Sarah and Ethan were their best hope for finally breaking the Covenant's power.

"Be careful," one of the villagers said. "And come back safe."

Sarah and Ethan nodded, their expressions resolute. "We will," Sarah promised.

They set off into the forest, the dense canopy of trees casting long shadows on the ground. The air was thick with the scent of pine and moss, and the only sounds were the rustling of leaves and the occasional chirping of birds. They followed the path marked on the map, their senses alert for any sign of danger.

As they ventured deeper into the forest, the atmosphere grew more oppressive. The trees seemed to close in around them, and the air grew colder. Sarah felt a strange energy in the air, as if they were being watched.

"Ethan, do you feel that?" Sarah asked, her voice barely above a whisper.

Ethan nodded, his eyes scanning the forest. "Yes. We're getting close."

They continued on, their path winding through the dense underbrush. After several hours of walking, they came upon a clearing. In the center of the clearing stood a large, ancient stone archway covered in intricate runes. The archway pulsed with a dark energy, and the air around it seemed to shimmer.

"This must be it," Sarah said, her heart pounding in her chest. "The Infernal Gate."

Ethan approached the archway, his eyes narrowing as he studied the runes. "These runes... they're unlike anything I've ever seen. We need to decipher them to close the gate."

Sarah took a deep breath and held up the amulet Selene had given her. The amulet glowed with a faint light, and she felt a surge of energy coursing through her. She approached the archway, holding the amulet out before her.

As the light from the amulet touched the runes, they began to glow with a bright, white light. The runes shifted and rearranged themselves, forming a pattern that Sarah could read. She began to recite the incantation, her voice steady and clear.

"Infernal Gate, portal of darkness,
By ancient runes, I seal thee.
Close the path to the underworld,
And break the Covenant's hold on thee."

As she spoke the words, the air around the archway crackled with energy. The dark energy that had pulsed from the gate began to wane, and the archway glowed brighter. The ground beneath their feet trembled, and the trees around them seemed to sway with the force of the incantation.

Just as they neared the end of the incantation, a group of shadowy figures emerged from the forest, their eyes glowing with a malevolent light. It was clear that these were remnants of the Dark Covenant, determined to protect the gate.

"We have to stop them!" Ethan shouted, drawing his sword.

Sarah continued the incantation, her voice unwavering. She could feel the power of the amulet guiding her, and she knew that they were close to closing the gate. Ethan fought off the attackers, his movements swift and precise.

The leader of the group advanced on Sarah, his eyes filled with rage. "You will not close the gate!" he hissed, raising a dark blade.

Sarah focused on the incantation, trusting Ethan to protect her. She could feel the energy of the gate reaching a fever pitch, the runes glowing with an intense light.

Ethan blocked the leader's attack, their blades clashing with a loud clang. "Sarah, hurry!" he shouted, his voice strained with effort.

With a final surge of energy, Sarah spoke the last words of the incantation. The archway glowed with a blinding light, and the dark energy that had pulsed from the gate dissipated into the air. The ground shook violently, and the archway began to crumble.

The leader of the group screamed in rage as the gate closed, his form disintegrating into nothingness. The remaining attackers fled into the forest, their power broken.

As the dust settled, Sarah and Ethan stood together, their hearts filled with a mixture of exhaustion and triumph. The Infernal Gate had been closed, and the power of the Dark Covenant was finally broken.

"We did it," Sarah said, her voice trembling with relief.

Ethan nodded, his expression filled with pride. "Yes, we did. The village is safe."

They made their way back to the village, the sense of peace and tranquility growing with each step. The villagers greeted them with cheers and tears of joy, their faces alight with gratitude and relief.

"Thank you," one of the villagers said. "You have saved us all."

Sarah and Ethan smiled, their hearts filled with a sense of fulfillment. They had faced the darkness and emerged victorious, their bond stronger than ever.

Over the next few weeks, the village of Raven's Hollow continued to rebuild and heal. The sense of community and resilience that had been forged in the face of adversity grew stronger with each passing day. Sarah continued to work alongside the villagers, using her knowledge and skills to help them create a brighter future.

The amulet, once a symbol of protection and hope, became a cherished heirloom, passed down through generations as a reminder of the strength and courage that had saved the village. Sarah wore it with pride, feeling its warmth and strength envelop her like a shield.

Despite the challenges they had faced, Sarah knew that the fight against the darkness had made them stronger. They had learned the value of unity, resilience, and the power of the human spirit. And as they looked to the future, they did so with hope and determination, ready to face whatever challenges lay ahead.

The journey had been long and difficult, but it had also been worth it. Sarah had found the story she had been searching for, and in the process, she had found herself. As she looked out over the village from the window of her room at the inn, she felt a sense of peace and fulfillment. The road ahead would undoubtedly bring new adventures, but she was ready to face them head-on.

AND WITH THAT THOUGHT, she turned to face the future with hope and determination, ready to uncover the truth and bring light to the darkest corners of the world.

Chapter 11: The Sacrifice

Sarah's discovery of the Infernal Gate had initially brought a sense of triumph and relief to the villagers of Raven's Hollow. The portal to the underworld, controlled by the Dark Covenant, was believed to be closed, severing the connection that fed their malevolent power. But as Sarah delved deeper into the ancient texts and manuscripts, she uncovered a horrifying truth: the gate's closure was temporary, and its seal required a sacrifice.

The words from the manuscript echoed in her mind, their meaning clear and undeniable:

"The Infernal Gate, once closed, will remain so only through the blood of the chosen. The sacrifice of the prophesied one, marked by destiny, shall seal the portal and break the curse forever."

THE REALIZATION THAT she was the prophesied sacrifice hit Sarah like a physical blow. Her heart pounded in her chest, and her breath came in short, ragged gasps. The weight of her destiny pressed down on her, threatening to crush her under its unbearable burden.

Sarah spent the next few days in a state of numb shock, grappling with the implications of her fate. The villagers, oblivious to the dire secret she carried, went about their lives, grateful for the peace they believed had been secured. She watched them with a heavy heart, knowing that their safety depended on her ultimate sacrifice.

Ethan noticed the change in Sarah's demeanor. He had come to know her well over the past months, and he could see the turmoil that churned beneath her calm exterior. One evening, as the sun dipped below the horizon, casting long shadows over the village, he approached her with concern etched on his face.

"Sarah, what's wrong?" he asked gently. "You've been distant lately. Did you find something in the texts?"

Sarah looked at him, her eyes filled with a sorrow that cut him to the core. She took a deep breath, trying to steady her voice. "Ethan, there's something I need to tell you. Something terrible."

Ethan's heart skipped a beat. "What is it?"

Sarah hesitated, struggling to find the words. "I found a passage in one of the manuscripts. It says that the Infernal Gate can only be permanently sealed through the sacrifice of the prophesied one. And... I believe I am that sacrifice."

Ethan's eyes widened in shock. "No. There has to be another way. We've fought too hard, come too far. We can't lose you."

Sarah shook her head, tears streaming down her face. "I wish there was another way, but the texts are clear. My sacrifice is the only thing that will keep the gate closed and protect the village."

Ethan's expression hardened with resolve. "I won't let you do this, Sarah. We'll find another way. I'll protect you, no matter what."

Sarah placed a hand on his cheek, her heart breaking at the pain she saw in his eyes. "Ethan, I don't want to die. But if it's the only way to keep the village safe, I have to do it. These people deserve a future free from the darkness."

Ethan pulled her into his arms, holding her tightly as they both wept. The reality of their situation was crushing, but their love for each other gave them strength.

The next morning, Sarah and Ethan began their search for an alternative solution in earnest. They pored over every ancient text and manuscript they could find, consulted with the villagers, and even reached out to neighboring towns for any hidden knowledge or forgotten lore. Despite their relentless efforts, the grim reality remained unchanged: the sacrifice was necessary.

As the days passed, Sarah found herself grappling with the moral implications of her fate. She had always believed in the power of the human spirit, in the ability to overcome darkness and create a better future. The thought of sacrificing herself to achieve that future was a bitter pill to swallow.

One evening, as she sat alone in her room at the inn, she stared at the amulet Selene had given her. The weight of her destiny pressed down on her, and she felt a deep sense of sorrow. She had come to love the village and its people, and the thought of leaving them behind filled her with anguish.

Ethan entered the room, his expression weary but determined. "Sarah, we need to talk."

She looked up, her eyes red from crying. "I know, Ethan. I know what you're going to say."

He sat down beside her, taking her hand in his. "I can't let you do this, Sarah. There has to be another way."

Sarah shook her head, tears streaming down her face. "We've looked everywhere, Ethan. There isn't another way. My sacrifice is the only thing that will keep the gate closed and protect the village."

Ethan's voice broke with emotion. "I can't lose you, Sarah. I love you."

The words hung in the air, heavy with the weight of their meaning. Sarah felt a surge of love and sorrow. "I love you too, Ethan. But sometimes, loving someone means letting them go."

Ethan pulled her into his arms, holding her tightly as they both wept. The reality of their situation was crushing, but their love for each other gave them strength.

The night before the sacrificial ritual, the village gathered to honor Sarah's bravery and selflessness. They held a ceremony in the village square, lighting candles and sharing stories of hope and resilience. The villagers' gratitude and love for Sarah were palpable, and she felt a deep sense of peace knowing that her sacrifice would give them a future.

As the ceremony came to a close, Sarah stood before the villagers, her heart filled with a mixture of sorrow and resolve. "Thank you," she said, her voice strong and clear. "Thank you for giving me a home, for showing me the power of community and love. I do this not out of duty, but out of love for all of you. My sacrifice will ensure that you have the future you deserve."

The villagers wept and cheered, their voices a chorus of gratitude and sorrow. Sarah felt their strength and love envelop her, giving her the courage to face her destiny.

The next morning, as the sun began to rise, Sarah and Ethan made their way to the clearing where the Infernal Gate stood. The ancient stone archway loomed before them, its runes glowing faintly in the early morning light. The air was thick with an oppressive energy, and the ground seemed to tremble with anticipation.

Ethan held Sarah's hand, his grip strong and reassuring. "I'm here with you, Sarah. Until the end."

Sarah nodded, her heart filled with love and determination. "Thank you, Ethan. I couldn't do this without you."

They approached the archway, the amulet glowing brightly in Sarah's hand. She began to recite the incantation, her voice steady and clear. The air around them crackled with energy, and the runes on the archway pulsed with a bright, white light.

As she spoke the final words, the ground beneath their feet shook violently, and the archway glowed with a blinding light. Sarah felt a surge of energy course through her, and she knew that the moment had come.

"Ethan, promise me you'll take care of the village," Sarah said, her voice trembling with emotion. "Promise me you'll keep them safe."

Ethan's eyes were filled with tears. "I promise, Sarah. I'll protect them with my life."

With a final, loving look at Ethan, Sarah stepped into the archway. The light enveloped her, and she felt a strange sense of peace wash over her. The darkness that had plagued the village for so long seemed to dissipate, and she knew that her sacrifice had succeeded.

As the light faded, the archway crumbled to the ground, the Infernal Gate finally sealed. Ethan fell to his knees, his heart breaking with the loss of the woman he loved. But he knew that her sacrifice had given the village a future free from darkness.

The villagers gathered in the clearing, their faces filled with grief and gratitude. They honored Sarah's memory with a solemn ceremony, vowing to carry on her legacy of hope and resilience.

Ethan returned to the village, his heart heavy with sorrow but filled with a renewed sense of purpose. He knew that he had to honor Sarah's sacrifice by protecting the village and ensuring that her legacy lived on.

Over the next few years, the village of Raven's Hollow flourished. The oppressive shadow of the Dark Covenant was a distant memory, and the villagers worked together to build a future filled with hope and possibility. They honored Sarah's memory with an annual festival, celebrating her bravery and selflessness.

Ethan became a leader in the village, guiding the villagers with the same strength and compassion that Sarah had shown. He wore the amulet she had given him as a symbol of their love and the bond they had shared.

Despite the challenges they faced, the villagers knew that they were stronger together. They had learned the value of unity, resilience, and the power of the human spirit. And as they looked to the future, they did so with hope and determination, ready to face whatever challenges lay ahead.

Sarah's sacrifice had given them a future, and they vowed to honor her memory by living their lives with the same courage and compassion she had shown. The journey had been long and difficult, but it had also been worth it. Sarah had found the story she had been searching for, and in the process, she had found herself. As she looked out over the village from the window of her room at the inn, she felt a sense of peace and fulfillment. The road ahead would undoubtedly bring new adventures, but she was ready to face them head-on.

And with that thought, she turned to face the future with hope and determination, ready to uncover the truth and bring light to the darkest corners of the world.

Chapter 12: The Final Gathering

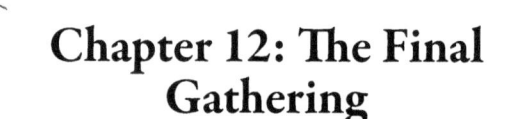

The tranquility that had settled over Raven's Hollow was shattered when whispers of a final, powerful ritual by the remnants of the Dark Covenant began to circulate. Despite Sarah's ultimate sacrifice to seal the Infernal Gate, it appeared that the Covenant had found a way to regroup and harness their dark energies once more. The villagers, who had tasted freedom and peace, were filled with dread at the prospect of the Covenant's return.

Ethan knew they couldn't afford to let the Covenant succeed in their dark endeavors. He had sworn to protect the village, and now, more than ever, he needed to honor Sarah's memory by preventing the Covenant's final ritual. The villagers, too, were determined to stand against the darkness that threatened to consume their lives once again.

One evening, as the sun set behind the mountains, casting long shadows over the village, Ethan gathered a group of trusted villagers in the village square. They included those who had proven themselves loyal and brave during the previous battles against the Covenant. Among them were Thomas, a skilled blacksmith; Lydia, a healer with knowledge of ancient herbs and remedies; and Marcus, a former member of the Covenant who had defected to fight against their tyranny.

"We've received word that the Dark Covenant is planning their final, most powerful ritual," Ethan began, his voice steady but urgent. "If they succeed, it could spell disaster for Raven's Hollow and beyond. We need to stop them once and for all."

Thomas stepped forward, his expression determined. "What do we know about this ritual, Ethan?"

Ethan glanced at Marcus, who nodded and spoke up. "The ritual is called the Convergence of Shadows. It's a ceremony designed to draw power from the underworld and unleash it upon the world of the living. The Covenant's leader, a powerful sorcerer named Malachi, is the key to the ritual. If we can stop him, we can prevent the ritual from being completed."

Lydia's eyes widened in concern. "But Malachi is incredibly powerful. How can we hope to defeat him?"

Ethan took a deep breath. "We have something they don't—unity and the will to protect our home. We also have the knowledge that Sarah left us. She believed in the power of the human spirit, and we need to channel that belief into our actions."

The group nodded in agreement, their resolve strengthening. They began to formulate a plan to infiltrate the Covenant's gathering and disrupt the ritual. They would use their combined skills and knowledge to outmaneuver the Covenant and bring Malachi to justice.

As they prepared for the mission, Ethan couldn't help but feel a mix of sorrow and determination. Sarah's sacrifice had been a turning point, and he was determined to honor her memory by ensuring that the Covenant was defeated once and for all. He knew that the road ahead would be fraught with danger, but he also knew that they had the strength to prevail.

The night of the final gathering arrived, and the group set out under the cover of darkness. They moved silently through the forest, their senses alert for any sign of danger. The air was thick with tension, and the sounds of the night seemed to amplify their anxiety.

As they approached the location where the ritual was to take place, they saw the glow of torches and heard the low murmur of voices. The Covenant had gathered in a large clearing, their robed figures moving in a rhythmic dance around a central altar. At the head of the altar stood Malachi, his presence radiating dark power.

Ethan signaled for the group to halt and crouched behind a large tree, surveying the scene. "We need to move quickly and quietly," he whispered. "Our goal is to disrupt the ritual and take down Malachi. Thomas, you and Lydia take the left flank. Marcus and I will take the right. Wait for my signal."

The group nodded in understanding and split into their designated positions. Ethan felt his heart pound in his chest as he watched the ritual unfold. The Covenant members chanted in unison, their voices rising and falling in a hypnotic cadence. The air crackled with dark energy, and Ethan knew they had to act fast.

With a deep breath, Ethan signaled for the attack. The group sprang into action, moving swiftly and silently through the underbrush. They closed in on the clearing, their weapons ready and their hearts filled with determination.

Ethan and Marcus reached the edge of the clearing and saw Malachi at the center of the ritual, his eyes closed in concentration. Ethan knew that their best chance was to take him by surprise and disrupt his focus.

"Now!" Ethan shouted, leaping into the clearing with Marcus at his side.

The Covenant members turned in shock as Ethan and Marcus charged forward, their weapons slicing through the air. The ritual was thrown into chaos, the chanting faltering as the attackers made their presence known.

Thomas and Lydia joined the fray from the left flank, their combined skills making quick work of the startled Covenant members. Lydia used her knowledge of herbs to create smoke bombs that disoriented their enemies, while Thomas's strength and precision with his sword cut through the opposition.

Malachi's eyes snapped open, and he let out a roar of anger. He raised his hands, and a wave of dark energy erupted from the altar, sending Ethan and Marcus sprawling to the ground. Ethan felt a searing pain in his chest as the dark energy washed over him, but he forced himself to stand and face Malachi.

"You think you can stop me?" Malachi sneered, his voice dripping with contempt. "You are nothing but insects compared to my power."

Ethan gritted his teeth, his resolve unwavering. "We're here to protect our home and the people we love. Your darkness has no place here."

Malachi laughed, a cold and hollow sound. "You are fools. The Convergence of Shadows cannot be stopped."

Ethan glanced at Marcus, who nodded in understanding. They needed to work together to take down Malachi. With a silent signal, they charged at the sorcerer, their movements coordinated and precise.

Malachi raised his hands again, but this time, Ethan and Marcus were ready. They dodged the wave of dark energy and closed the distance between them and their target. Ethan swung his sword at Malachi, but the sorcerer deflected the blow with a shield of dark energy.

"You cannot defeat me!" Malachi hissed, his eyes blazing with fury.

Ethan felt a surge of frustration, but he refused to give up. He glanced around the clearing and saw Thomas and Lydia making their way toward them, their faces set with determination.

"Lydia, the herbs!" Ethan shouted.

Lydia nodded and threw a pouch of herbs into the air. The herbs exploded in a cloud of smoke, enveloping Malachi and obscuring his vision. Ethan took advantage of the distraction and lunged at the sorcerer, his sword slicing through the dark energy shield.

Malachi let out a howl of rage and pain as the blade struck him. He stumbled backward, his concentration broken. The dark energy that had surrounded him began to dissipate, and the ritual was thrown into disarray.

"Now, Thomas!" Ethan shouted.

Thomas charged forward, his sword gleaming in the torchlight. He swung the blade with all his strength, striking Malachi and sending him crashing to the ground. The sorcerer lay motionless, his power broken.

The remaining Covenant members looked on in shock and fear, their leader defeated. They began to retreat, their dark energy fading as they fled into the forest. The clearing was filled with an eerie silence, the once powerful ritual now a distant memory.

Ethan felt a wave of relief wash over him as he looked at his companions. They had succeeded. The Dark Covenant's final ritual had been stopped, and Malachi had been defeated.

"Is it over?" Lydia asked, her voice trembling with emotion.

Ethan nodded, his heart swelling with pride. "Yes, it's over. The Covenant is finished."

The group embraced, their faces filled with relief and gratitude. They had faced the darkness and emerged victorious, their bond stronger than ever.

As they made their way back to the village, the villagers greeted them with cheers and tears of joy. They had been anxiously awaiting news of the battle, and their faces lit up with relief as they saw their protectors return safely.

Ethan addressed the villagers, his voice filled with pride and determination. "The Dark Covenant has been defeated. Their power is broken, and they will no longer threaten our home. We have fought hard and sacrificed much, but we have prevailed. Let us honor the memory of those we have lost and look to the future with hope and resilience."

The villagers erupted into cheers, their voices a chorus of gratitude and celebration. They knew that their home was safe, and they vowed to honor the memory of those who had fought to protect them.

In the days that followed, the village of Raven's Hollow continued to rebuild and heal. The sense of community and resilience that had been forged in the face of adversity grew stronger with each passing day. The villagers worked together to create a future filled with hope and possibility, their hearts filled with gratitude for the bravery and selflessness of those who had protected them.

Ethan, Thomas, Lydia, and Marcus remained pillars of strength and leadership in the village. They guided the villagers with the same determination and compassion that had carried them through the darkest of times. They honored the memory of Sarah and all those who had sacrificed to protect their home, their legacy a beacon of hope for future generations.

The amulet that Sarah had given Ethan became a cherished heirloom, passed down through generations as a reminder of the strength and courage that had saved the village. Ethan wore it with pride, feeling its warmth and strength envelop him like a shield.

Despite the challenges they had faced, the villagers knew that they were stronger together. They had learned the value of unity, resilience, and the power of the human spirit. And as they looked to the future, they did so with hope and determination, ready to face whatever challenges lay ahead.

Sarah's sacrifice had given them a future, and they vowed to honor her memory by living their lives with the same courage and compassion she had shown. The journey had been long and difficult, but it had also been worth it. Sarah had found the story she had been searching for, and in the process, she had found herself. As she looked out over the village from the window of her room at the inn, she felt a sense of peace and fulfillment. The road ahead would undoubtedly bring new adventures, but she was ready to face them head-on.

And with that thought, she turned to face the future with hope and determination, ready to uncover the truth and bring light to the darkest corners of the world.

In the quiet moments that followed the defeat of the Dark Covenant, Ethan and his companions took time to reflect on the journey they had undertaken. They had faced unimaginable challenges and had come through stronger and more united. They had learned the value of trust, sacrifice, and the indomitable power of the human spirit.

As they stood together in the village square, the dawn of a new day breaking over the horizon, Ethan felt a deep sense of peace. The darkness had been vanquished, and a new era of hope and resilience had begun. They had honored Sarah's memory, and in doing so, they had ensured that her legacy would live on.

The final gathering of the Dark Covenant had been their last stand, and they had been defeated. The villagers of Raven's Hollow could now look to the future with hope and determination, knowing that they were protected by the strength and unity they had forged in the face of adversity.

As Ethan looked out over the village, he felt a renewed sense of purpose. The journey was not over, and there would be new challenges to face. But he knew that they would face them together, with the same courage and determination that had carried them through the darkest of times.

The village of Raven's Hollow had become a beacon of hope, a testament to the power of unity and resilience. And as they moved forward, they did so with the knowledge that they were stronger together, ready to face whatever the future held.

Ethan felt a sense of peace as he stood with his friends and companions, knowing that they had honored Sarah's memory and ensured that her sacrifice had not been in vain. The road ahead would undoubtedly bring new adventures, but they were ready to face them head-on, united in their determination to protect their home and the people they loved.

With the dawn of a new day, they looked to the future with hope and resilience, ready to uncover the truth and bring light to the darkest corners of the world.

Chapter 13: The Battle for Souls

The peace that had settled over Raven's Hollow was but a fragile veneer. Whispers of the Dark Covenant's impending return grew louder, and the villagers sensed the brewing storm. The final battle was imminent, and they knew they had to prepare for the ultimate confrontation. The fate of their home and the souls of their loved ones hung in the balance.

Ethan, now the village's stalwart leader, convened a meeting in the village square. The trusted allies who had fought alongside him—Thomas, Lydia, Marcus, and others—gathered, their faces etched with determination and resolve. The weight of Sarah's sacrifice and the knowledge that they might be the village's last line of defense pressed heavily upon them.

"We've received reliable information that the Dark Covenant is planning a climactic ritual to reclaim their lost power," Ethan began, his voice steady despite the tension in the air. "This ritual will be their most powerful yet, designed to enslave the souls of our people and bind them to the underworld. We cannot let this happen."

Thomas, the blacksmith, spoke up, his deep voice resonating with resolve. "What do we know about their plans?"

Ethan glanced at Marcus, who had used his knowledge as a former member of the Covenant to gather crucial intelligence. "The ritual requires a convergence of supernatural forces," Marcus explained. "They plan to summon and bind these forces at a nexus point located in the heart of the forest, where the energy is most potent. They'll be protected by powerful wards and dark enchantments."

Lydia, the healer, looked concerned. "How do we break through those wards?"

"We have something they don't," Ethan said, his gaze shifting to the amulet that Sarah had given him. "Sarah left us with the knowledge and tools to fight this darkness. The amulet she gave me, combined with the wisdom in the manuscripts, holds the key to disrupting their magic."

Ethan's words infused the group with a renewed sense of hope and determination. They knew that Sarah's legacy and sacrifice had provided them with the means to confront the Covenant. Together, they formulated a plan to infiltrate the Covenant's stronghold, disrupt the ritual, and defeat their leader, Malachi, once and for all.

As night fell, the villagers prepared for the battle ahead. Weapons were sharpened, protective charms and potions were distributed, and wards were placed around the village to safeguard those who would remain behind. The air was thick with anticipation and the knowledge that this battle would determine their fate.

Ethan led his group into the forest, moving silently through the dense underbrush. The night was dark, the moon obscured by heavy clouds, casting an ominous pall over the landscape. The forest, usually a place of tranquility, seemed alive with a malevolent energy, as if it knew the darkness that was about to unfold.

As they neared the nexus point, the glow of torches and the sound of chanting reached their ears. Ethan signaled for the group to halt and crouched behind a large tree, surveying the scene. The Covenant had gathered in a large clearing, their robed figures moving in a rhythmic dance around a central altar. At the head of the altar stood Malachi, his presence radiating dark power.

Ethan whispered to his companions, "We need to move quickly and disrupt the ritual. Lydia, you and Thomas will take the left flank. Marcus and I will take the right. Wait for my signal."

The group nodded in understanding and split into their designated positions. Ethan's heart pounded as he watched the ritual unfold. The Covenant members chanted in unison, their voices rising and falling in a hypnotic cadence. The air crackled with dark energy, and Ethan knew they had to act fast.

With a deep breath, Ethan signaled for the attack. The group sprang into action, moving swiftly and silently through the underbrush. They closed in on the clearing, their weapons ready and their hearts filled with determination.

Ethan and Marcus reached the edge of the clearing and saw Malachi at the center of the ritual, his eyes closed in concentration. Ethan knew that their best chance was to take him by surprise and disrupt his focus.

"Now!" Ethan shouted, leaping into the clearing with Marcus at his side.

The Covenant members turned in shock as Ethan and Marcus charged forward, their weapons slicing through the air. The ritual was thrown into chaos, the chanting faltering as the attackers made their presence known.

Thomas and Lydia joined the fray from the left flank, their combined skills making quick work of the startled Covenant members. Lydia used her knowledge of herbs to create smoke bombs that disoriented their enemies, while Thomas's strength and precision with his sword cut through the opposition.

Malachi's eyes snapped open, and he let out a roar of anger. He raised his hands, and a wave of dark energy erupted from the altar, sending Ethan and Marcus sprawling to the ground. Ethan felt a searing pain in his chest as the dark energy washed over him, but he forced himself to stand and face Malachi.

"You think you can stop me?" Malachi sneered, his voice dripping with contempt. "You are nothing but insects compared to my power."

Ethan gritted his teeth, his resolve unwavering. "We're here to protect our home and the people we love. Your darkness has no place here."

Malachi laughed, a cold and hollow sound. "You are fools. The Convergence of Shadows cannot be stopped."

Ethan glanced at Marcus, who nodded in understanding. They needed to work together to take down Malachi. With a silent signal, they charged at the sorcerer, their movements coordinated and precise.

Malachi raised his hands again, but this time, Ethan and Marcus were ready. They dodged the wave of dark energy and closed the distance between them and their target. Ethan swung his sword at Malachi, but the sorcerer deflected the blow with a shield of dark energy.

"You cannot defeat me!" Malachi hissed, his eyes blazing with fury.

Ethan felt a surge of frustration, but he refused to give up. He glanced around the clearing and saw Thomas and Lydia making their way toward them, their faces set with determination.

"Lydia, the herbs!" Ethan shouted.

Lydia nodded and threw a pouch of herbs into the air. The herbs exploded in a cloud of smoke, enveloping Malachi and obscuring his vision. Ethan took advantage of the distraction and lunged at the sorcerer, his sword slicing through the dark energy shield.

Malachi let out a howl of rage and pain as the blade struck him. He stumbled backward, his concentration broken. The dark energy that had surrounded him began to dissipate, and the ritual was thrown into disarray.

"Now, Thomas!" Ethan shouted.

Thomas charged forward, his sword gleaming in the torchlight. He swung the blade with all his strength, striking Malachi and sending him crashing to the ground. The sorcerer lay motionless, his power broken.

The remaining Covenant members looked on in shock and fear, their leader defeated. They began to retreat, their dark energy fading as they fled into the forest. The clearing was filled with an eerie silence, the once powerful ritual now a distant memory.

Ethan felt a wave of relief wash over him as he looked at his companions. They had succeeded. The Dark Covenant's final ritual had been stopped, and Malachi had been defeated.

"Is it over?" Lydia asked, her voice trembling with emotion.

Ethan nodded, his heart swelling with pride. "Yes, it's over. The Covenant is finished."

The group embraced, their faces filled with relief and gratitude. They had faced the darkness and emerged victorious, their bond stronger than ever.

As they made their way back to the village, the villagers greeted them with cheers and tears of joy. They had been anxiously awaiting news of the battle, and their faces lit up with relief as they saw their protectors return safely.

Ethan addressed the villagers, his voice filled with pride and determination. "The Dark Covenant has been defeated. Their power is broken, and they will no longer threaten our home. We have fought hard and sacrificed much, but we have prevailed. Let us honor the memory of those we have lost and look to the future with hope and resilience."

The villagers erupted into cheers, their voices a chorus of gratitude and celebration. They knew that their home was safe, and they vowed to honor the memory of those who had fought to protect them.

In the days that followed, the village of Raven's Hollow continued to rebuild and heal. The sense of community and resilience that had been forged in the face of adversity grew stronger with each passing day. The villagers worked together to create a future filled with hope and possibility, their hearts filled with gratitude for the bravery and selflessness of those who had protected them.

Ethan, Thomas, Lydia, and Marcus remained pillars of strength and leadership in the village. They guided the villagers with the same determination and compassion that had carried them through the darkest of times. They honored the memory of Sarah and all those who had sacrificed to protect their home, their legacy a beacon of hope for future generations.

The amulet that Sarah had given Ethan became a cherished heirloom, passed down through generations as a reminder of the strength and courage that had saved the village. Ethan wore it with pride, feeling its warmth and strength envelop him like a shield.

Despite the challenges they had faced, the villagers knew that they were stronger together. They had learned the value of unity, resilience, and the power of the human spirit. And as they looked to the future, they did so with hope and determination, ready to face whatever challenges lay ahead.

Sarah's sacrifice had given them a future, and they vowed to honor her memory by living their lives with the same courage and compassion she had shown. The journey had been long and difficult, but it had also been worth it. Sarah

had found the story she had been searching for, and in the process, she had found herself. As she looked out over the village from the window of her room at the inn, she felt a sense of peace and fulfillment. The road ahead would undoubtedly bring new adventures, but she was ready to face them head-on.

And with that thought, she turned to face the future with hope and determination, ready to uncover the truth and bring light to the darkest corners of the world.

In the quiet moments that followed the defeat of the Dark Covenant, Ethan and his companions took time to reflect on the journey they had undertaken. They had faced unimaginable challenges and had come through stronger and more united. They had learned the value of trust, sacrifice, and the indomitable power of the human spirit.

As they stood together in the village square, the dawn of a new day breaking over the horizon, Ethan felt a deep sense of peace. The darkness had been vanquished, and a new era of hope and resilience had begun. They had honored Sarah's memory, and in doing so, they had ensured that her legacy would live on.

The final gathering of the Dark Covenant had been their last stand, and they had been defeated. The villagers of Raven's Hollow could now look to the future with hope and determination, knowing that they were protected by the strength and unity they had forged in the face of adversity.

As Ethan looked out over the village, he felt a renewed sense of purpose. The journey was not over, and there would be new challenges to face. But he knew that they would face them together, with the same courage and determination that had carried them through the darkest of times.

The village of Raven's Hollow had become a beacon of hope, a testament to the power of unity and resilience. And as they moved forward, they did so with the knowledge that they were stronger together, ready to face whatever the future held.

Ethan felt a sense of peace as he stood with his friends and companions, knowing that they had honored Sarah's memory and ensured that her sacrifice had not been in vain. The road ahead would undoubtedly bring new adventures, but they were ready to face them head-on, united in their determination to protect their home and the people they loved.

With the dawn of a new day, they looked to the future with hope and resilience, ready to uncover the truth and bring light to the darkest corners of the world.

Chapter 14: The Collapse

The village of Raven's Hollow had enjoyed a fragile peace since the climactic battle against the Dark Covenant. The community had begun to heal, and hope was slowly taking root in the hearts of the villagers. However, beneath the surface of this newfound tranquility, an ancient and malevolent force was stirring.

One night, a low rumbling sound emanated from deep within the forest. It reverberated through the village, shaking the foundations of homes and waking the villagers from their slumber. Fear spread quickly as people rushed out of their houses, their eyes filled with dread.

Ethan, who had been on guard ever since the defeat of the Covenant, immediately sensed that something was terribly wrong. He gathered his trusted allies—Thomas, Lydia, and Marcus—and they headed toward the source of the disturbance.

As they approached the clearing where the Infernal Gate had once stood, the ground began to tremble violently. The ancient stone archway, which had collapsed after Sarah's sacrifice, now seemed to pulse with a dark energy. The air around it shimmered with an otherworldly light, and the runes etched into the stones glowed ominously.

Lydia's eyes widened with horror. "The gate... it's trying to reopen!"

Ethan clenched his fists, his mind racing. "We need to stop it. If the gate collapses completely, it will consume the entire village."

Thomas, ever the pragmatist, looked around for any sign of a solution. "We need to stabilize it somehow. There must be something in the manuscripts that can help us."

Marcus nodded, his face grim. "I'll go back to the village and bring the texts. Maybe there's something we missed."

As Marcus sprinted back to the village, Ethan, Thomas, and Lydia tried to assess the situation. The ground around the gate continued to shake, and dark tendrils of energy began to seep from the cracks in the stones. The air grew colder, and an oppressive sense of dread filled the clearing.

Ethan held up the amulet that Sarah had given him, hoping it might offer some protection. The amulet glowed with a faint light, but it was clear that its power alone would not be enough to stop the impending catastrophe.

"We need to buy Marcus some time," Ethan said, his voice steady despite the fear gnawing at him. "Thomas, Lydia, help me fortify the area. We'll use whatever we can find to create a barrier."

The three of them worked quickly, gathering rocks, branches, and anything else that might help contain the dark energy. They placed the makeshift barriers around the gate, hoping to slow its collapse long enough for Marcus to return with the necessary knowledge.

Minutes felt like hours as they struggled against the malevolent force. The ground trembled more violently, and the dark energy continued to grow stronger. Just as their efforts seemed futile, Marcus returned, breathless and carrying a stack of ancient manuscripts.

"I found something!" Marcus shouted, handing the texts to Ethan. "There's a passage about stabilizing portals. It mentions a ritual, but it requires a great sacrifice."

Ethan's heart sank as he read the passage. The ritual required the life force of a willing participant to bind the gate and prevent its collapse. The realization hit him like a physical blow: another sacrifice was needed, and there was no time to find another way.

Lydia, reading over Ethan's shoulder, gasped. "We can't ask someone to do this. It's too much."

Ethan's mind raced, memories of Sarah's sacrifice flooding back. He knew what had to be done, but the thought of losing another loved one was almost unbearable.

"We have to try," Ethan said, his voice filled with resolve. "If we don't, the entire village will be lost."

The group fell silent, the weight of the decision pressing down on them. Finally, Ethan took a deep breath and stepped forward. "I'll do it. I'll be the one to make the sacrifice."

Thomas and Lydia stared at him in shock. "No, Ethan," Thomas said, his voice shaking. "We can't let you do this. There has to be another way."

Ethan shook his head, his eyes filled with determination. "There isn't. The village needs to be saved, and I'm willing to do whatever it takes."

Before anyone could protest further, Ethan began to recite the incantation from the manuscript. The ground beneath him glowed with a bright light, and the air crackled with energy. He felt a surge of power course through him, and he knew that his life force was being drawn into the ritual.

As the incantation continued, the dark energy from the gate began to recede. The trembling ground started to stabilize, and the oppressive sense of dread lifted slightly. But Ethan knew that the ritual was far from complete. The gate required a sustained flow of life force to be fully stabilized.

Lydia, tears streaming down her face, reached out to Ethan. "Please, there has to be another way. We can't lose you too."

Ethan's eyes softened as he looked at his friends. "This is the only way. You all need to be strong and carry on. Protect the village and honor Sarah's memory."

Just as the ritual reached its climax, a blinding light enveloped the clearing. Ethan felt a strange sense of peace wash over him, and he knew that his sacrifice was working. The dark energy from the gate continued to recede, and the ground stabilized further.

But then, something unexpected happened. The amulet around Ethan's neck began to glow with an intense light, and a voice echoed in his mind.

"Ethan, no. It is not your time."

The voice was familiar, filled with warmth and love. It was Sarah's voice. Ethan felt a surge of emotions—hope, sorrow, and a renewed determination.

"Sarah?" Ethan whispered, his voice trembling.

"Yes, Ethan. I am here. Your sacrifice is not necessary. There is another way."

Ethan felt the energy of the amulet course through him, and the ritual's demand on his life force began to lessen. The glow of the amulet intensified, and the dark energy around the gate continued to recede.

"Use the amulet and the knowledge in the manuscripts," Sarah's voice guided him. "There is a way to stabilize the gate without sacrificing yourself."

Ethan, filled with renewed hope, began to chant a different incantation, one that combined the power of the amulet with the ancient knowledge in the manuscripts. The light from the amulet enveloped the clearing, and the dark energy around the gate was pushed back even further.

Thomas, Lydia, and Marcus watched in awe as Ethan's chant grew stronger. The ground around the gate stabilized completely, and the oppressive sense of dread lifted entirely.

Ethan felt Sarah's presence guiding him, and he knew that her spirit was still with him, protecting him and the village. With a final, powerful chant, the gate was sealed completely, its dark energy banished.

As the light from the amulet faded, Ethan collapsed to the ground, exhausted but alive. Thomas and Lydia rushed to his side, their faces filled with relief and gratitude.

"Ethan, you're alive!" Lydia cried, tears of joy streaming down her face.

Ethan nodded weakly, his heart filled with gratitude for Sarah's guidance. "Yes, thanks to Sarah. She showed me another way."

The group embraced, their hearts filled with hope and relief. The Infernal Gate was sealed, and the village of Raven's Hollow was safe once more.

As they made their way back to the village, the villagers greeted them with cheers and tears of joy. They had been anxiously awaiting news of the battle, and their faces lit up with relief as they saw their protectors return safely.

Ethan addressed the villagers, his voice filled with pride and determination. "The Infernal Gate has been sealed, and the Dark Covenant is no more. We have fought hard and sacrificed much, but we have prevailed. Let us honor the memory of those we have lost and look to the future with hope and resilience."

The villagers erupted into cheers, their voices a chorus of gratitude and celebration. They knew that their home was safe, and they vowed to honor the memory of those who had fought to protect them.

In the days that followed, the village of Raven's Hollow continued to rebuild and heal. The sense of community and resilience that had been forged in the face of adversity grew stronger with each passing day. The villagers worked together to create a future filled with hope and possibility, their hearts filled with gratitude for the bravery and selflessness of those who had protected them.

Ethan, Thomas, Lydia, and Marcus remained pillars of strength and leadership in the village. They guided the villagers with the same determination and compassion that had carried them through the darkest of times. They honored the memory of Sarah and all those who had sacrificed to protect their home, their legacy a beacon of hope for future generations.

The amulet that Sarah had given Ethan became a cherished heirloom, passed down through generations as a reminder of the strength and courage that had saved the village. Ethan wore it with pride, feeling its warmth and strength envelop him like a shield.

Despite the challenges they had faced, the villagers knew that they were stronger together. They had learned the value of unity, resilience, and the power of the human spirit. And as they looked to the future, they did so with hope and determination, ready to face whatever challenges lay ahead.

Sarah's sacrifice had given them a future, and they vowed to honor her memory by living their lives with the same courage and compassion she had shown. The journey had been long and difficult, but it had also been worth it. Sarah had found the story she had been searching for, and in the process, she had found herself. As she looked out over the village from the window of her room at the inn, she felt a sense of peace and fulfillment. The road ahead would undoubtedly bring new adventures, but she was ready to face them head-on.

And with that thought, she turned to face the future with hope and determination, ready to uncover the truth and bring light to the darkest corners of the world.

In the quiet moments that followed the defeat of the Dark Covenant, Ethan and his companions took time to reflect on the journey they had undertaken. They had faced unimaginable challenges and had come through stronger and more united. They had learned the value of trust, sacrifice, and the indomitable power of the human spirit.

As they stood together in the village square, the dawn of a new day breaking over the horizon, Ethan felt a deep sense of peace. The darkness had been vanquished, and a new era of hope and resilience had begun. They had honored Sarah's memory, and in doing so, they had ensured that her legacy would live on.

The final gathering of the Dark Covenant had been their last stand, and they had been defeated. The villagers of Raven's Hollow could now look to the future with hope and determination, knowing that they were protected by the strength and unity they had forged in the face of adversity.

As Ethan looked out over the village, he felt a renewed sense of purpose. The journey was not over, and there would be new challenges to face. But he knew that they would face them together, with the same courage and determination that had carried them through the darkest of times.

The village of Raven's Hollow had become a beacon of hope, a testament to the power of unity and resilience. And as they moved forward, they did so with the knowledge that they were stronger together, ready to face whatever the future held.

Ethan felt a sense of peace as he stood with his friends and companions, knowing that they had honored Sarah's memory and ensured that her sacrifice had not been in vain. The road ahead would undoubtedly bring new adventures, but they were ready to face them head-on, united in their determination to protect their home and the people they loved.

With the dawn of a new day, they looked to the future with hope and resilience, ready to uncover the truth and bring light to the darkest corners of the world.

Chapter 15: The Dawn of Hope

The first light of dawn broke over Raven's Hollow, casting a soft, golden glow over the village. The battle was over, but its impact still lingered in the air, a palpable reminder of the sacrifices made and the courage displayed. The villagers, weary but triumphant, began to emerge from their homes, ready to face the new day with a renewed sense of hope and resilience.

Ethan stood in the village square, his eyes scanning the horizon as the sun rose higher. The memories of the battle were fresh in his mind—the clash of swords, the surge of dark energy, and the triumphant moment when they had finally defeated the Dark Covenant. But his thoughts were also filled with concern for Sarah, who had played a crucial role in sealing the Infernal Gate and ensuring the village's safety.

As the villagers gathered around him, Ethan's heart swelled with pride and gratitude. They had fought bravely, united by a common goal, and now they stood together, ready to rebuild and heal. But amidst the joy and relief, there was also a sense of loss. They had all been changed by the events that had transpired, and they knew that the journey ahead would not be easy.

Lydia approached Ethan, her expression a mix of hope and worry. "How is Sarah?" she asked softly.

Ethan sighed, his gaze shifting to the inn where Sarah was resting. "She's alive, but the experience has left her changed. She's been through so much, and I can only hope that she finds the strength to heal."

Lydia nodded, her eyes filled with empathy. "She has always been strong, Ethan. She will find her way."

Thomas and Marcus joined them, their faces reflecting the same mixture of emotions. "The villagers are ready to help with the rebuilding," Thomas said. "We need to start by clearing the debris and fortifying the village defenses. We can't afford to be caught off guard again."

Ethan nodded in agreement. "Let's get to work. We have a lot to do, but I know we can do it together."

As the villagers set to work, clearing debris and repairing damaged structures, Ethan took a moment to check on Sarah. He entered the inn quietly, making his way to her room. She lay on the bed, her eyes closed, but her breathing steady. The amulet she had given him rested on the nightstand, a symbol of the strength and protection she had provided.

Ethan sat beside her, taking her hand in his. "Sarah," he whispered, his voice filled with emotion. "We did it. The village is safe, thanks to you."

Sarah's eyes fluttered open, and she looked up at him with a weak smile. "Ethan," she murmured. "I'm so glad you're here."

Ethan squeezed her hand gently. "I was so worried about you. You've been through so much."

Sarah nodded slowly, her eyes reflecting the depth of her experiences. "I feel... different. Like a part of me has changed forever. But I'm alive, and that's what matters."

Ethan leaned in closer, his voice filled with determination. "We're going to get through this, Sarah. Together. The village is rebuilding, and we have a future to look forward to. You've given us that."

Tears welled up in Sarah's eyes as she looked at Ethan. "Thank you, Ethan. For everything."

As the days turned into weeks, the village of Raven's Hollow slowly began to heal. The physical scars of the battle were repaired, and the emotional wounds started to mend. The villagers, united by their shared experiences, worked tirelessly to rebuild their homes and their lives.

Sarah, though still recovering, found solace in writing. She decided to document her experiences, to ensure that the truth of what had happened was known and remembered. She spent hours each day in the inn's small study, surrounded by manuscripts and journals, pouring her heart and soul into her writing.

Ethan, ever supportive, would often join her, offering encouragement and helping her recall details of their journey. Together, they revisited the memories of their battles, their triumphs, and their losses. It was a cathartic process for both of them, a way to make sense of the events that had changed their lives forever.

One evening, as the sun set over the village, casting a warm, golden light over everything, Sarah and Ethan sat together on the inn's porch. The manuscript, nearly complete, lay between them.

"I can't believe it's almost done," Sarah said, her voice filled with a mixture of relief and pride. "I never thought I'd be able to put it all into words."

Ethan smiled, his eyes reflecting his admiration for her. "You've done an incredible job, Sarah. This book will be a testament to everything we've been through and a beacon of hope for the future."

Sarah nodded, her heart swelling with emotion. "I just want people to know the truth. To remember the sacrifices that were made and the strength that we found in each other."

As the last rays of sunlight faded, casting the village into twilight, Sarah and Ethan sat in companionable silence, reflecting on their journey. The village had emerged from the darkness, and they had found a sense of peace and hope that had once seemed impossible.

The next morning, the village gathered in the square for a special ceremony. Sarah had requested that they commemorate the battle and honor the memory of those who had sacrificed their lives. It was a moment of reflection and gratitude, a chance to acknowledge the resilience and strength of the community.

Ethan stood beside Sarah as she addressed the villagers, her voice strong and clear. "Today, we come together to honor the memory of those we have lost and to celebrate the strength and unity that have brought us through the darkest of times. We have faced unimaginable challenges, but we have emerged stronger and more united. Let us never forget the sacrifices that were made and the courage that we found within ourselves."

The villagers listened with rapt attention, their faces reflecting a deep sense of pride and gratitude. They knew that they had been part of something extraordinary, a journey that had tested their limits and revealed their true strength.

As the ceremony came to a close, Sarah held up her manuscript, a symbol of their collective journey. "This book is not just my story," she said. "It is our story. A story of resilience, of hope, and of the indomitable power of the human spirit. Let us continue to move forward, together, and build a future filled with hope and possibility."

The villagers erupted into applause, their voices a chorus of gratitude and celebration. They knew that they had been part of something extraordinary, and they were determined to honor the legacy of those who had fought to protect them.

In the weeks that followed, the village continued to rebuild and heal. The sense of community and resilience that had been forged in the face of adversity grew stronger with each passing day. The villagers worked together to create a future filled with hope and possibility, their hearts filled with gratitude for the bravery and selflessness of those who had protected them.

Sarah's manuscript, once completed, became a cherished document, passed down through generations as a reminder of the strength and courage that had saved the village. It served as a beacon of hope and inspiration, a testament to the power of unity and resilience.

Ethan, Thomas, Lydia, and Marcus remained pillars of strength and leadership in the village. They guided the villagers with the same determination and compassion that had carried them through the darkest of times. They honored the memory of Sarah and all those who had sacrificed to protect their home, their legacy a beacon of hope for future generations.

Despite the challenges they had faced, the villagers knew that they were stronger together. They had learned the value of unity, resilience, and the power of the human spirit. And as they looked to the future, they did so with hope and determination, ready to face whatever challenges lay ahead.

Sarah's sacrifice had given them a future, and they vowed to honor her memory by living their lives with the same courage and compassion she had shown. The journey had been long and difficult, but it had also been worth it. Sarah had found the story she had been searching for, and in the process, she had found herself. As she looked out over the village from the window of her room at the inn, she felt a sense of peace and fulfillment. The road ahead would undoubtedly bring new adventures, but she was ready to face them head-on.

And with that thought, she turned to face the future with hope and determination, ready to uncover the truth and bring light to the darkest corners of the world.

The village of Raven's Hollow had become a beacon of hope, a testament to the power of unity and resilience. And as they moved forward, they did so with the knowledge that they were stronger together, ready to face whatever the future held.

Ethan felt a sense of peace as he stood with his friends and companions, knowing that they had honored Sarah's memory and ensured that her sacrifice had not been in vain. The road ahead would undoubtedly bring new adventures, but they were ready to face them head-on, united in their determination to protect their home and the people they loved.

With the dawn of a new day, they looked to the future with hope and resilience, ready to uncover the truth and bring light to the darkest corners of the world.

Don't miss out!

Visit the website below and you can sign up to receive emails whenever Samantha Marie Rodriguez publishes a new book. There's no charge and no obligation.

https://books2read.com/r/B-A-VXOXB-JUXIF

BOOKS2READ

Connecting independent readers to independent writers.

About the Author

Samantha Marie Rodriguez is a celebrated author specializing in occult and supernatural fiction. Her captivating stories explore the hidden realms of magic, mystery, and the unknown, drawing readers into worlds filled with enchantment and suspense. With a lifelong fascination for the supernatural, Samantha combines her extensive research and vivid imagination to create rich, immersive narratives. When she's not writing, she enjoys studying folklore, practicing tarot, and exploring haunted locales. Samantha's work has garnered a devoted following, making her a standout voice in the genre of occult and supernatural fiction.

Milton Keynes UK
Ingram Content Group UK Ltd.
UKHW042038031224
452078UK00001B/238